DATE			

AN OLD TALE CARVED OUT OF STONE

BY

A. LINEVSKI

Translated from the Russian by Maria Polushkin

CROWN PUBLISHERS, INC., NEW YORK

Printed in the United States of America
Library of Congress Catalog Card Number: 72–92386
ISBN: 0–517–50263–1
Published simultaneously in Canada by General Publishing Company Limited
First Edition

The text of this book is set in 11 pt. Times Roman.

For my husband, Ken, and all my family

AN OLD TALE CARVED OUT OF STONE

PART I

Chapter 1

EEEE-AAAA-OOOO . . . AAAA-OOOOO-EEEEE! A long wail sounded over the river, not clearly human, nor yet clearly animal. Trailing off, the sound was finally lost in the thicket of shaggy spruce trees that grew along the banks of the wide, deep river Vig.

Eeeaaaaoooiii! The wail came from the top of the rocky island, in the midst of a raging river which squeezed into a narrow divide, past the island, sometimes flying up in a million tiny drops, sometimes covered with thick billows of white foam.

On the island, on the highest part of a cliff overlooking the water, a dim fire burned. Long streams of pungent smoke curled upward from a smoldering heap of damp branches. A soft wind blew the smoke past the faces of the old women sitting around the fire. Near to a frenzy, the women were shouting, shaking their reedy old arms in the air. In front, an old woman knelt by the fire, her face painted with blood. Her gray hair was plaited into nine thin braids. A crown carved out of a deer skull, antlers attached, circled her head.

This was Fox Paw, the High Koldunya of the village. She was rubbing several small flat stones between her hands.

One by one they fell to the earth. "As the stones fall from my hands, so will deer fall out of the clouds onto the earth!" she sang in a wailing voice. The other women repeated her words in a chorus.

The High Koldunya picked up the stones from the ground and, closing her eyes tightly, threw them so that they bounced along the smooth rock face of the cliff and fell one by one into the water below. The Koldunya started singing once again, "Many deer in the forest there are. Our hunters will find and kill them." The other old women, the koldunyii, sang with her.

In the north, hunger was the official harbinger of spring, and this year, as in years past, the people of the village were hungry.

All day long the mournful wails of the hungry women could be heard above the roar of the rapids. Listening to their wails, the people of the village huddled in their dug-outs and recalled the bygone days of plenty. "We ate much then," they said again and again, "hunger was far from our minds."

Liok was an ordinary boy of fourteen summers, with a childish upturned nose and light eyes that sparkled with youthful enthusiasm. Like the other boys, he snatched sweet roots from the hands of the sadly squealing girls who had patiently dug them from the ground in the forest. He could catch a fish in the stream with his bare hands and would eat it raw as soon as he had caught it. With his keen sense of smell, he could find mushrooms in the forest and hidden nests that held delicious eggs. Fighting with other boys, he was, perhaps, not always the winner, but searching for molting ducks, he was unbeaten. No one among the other young people had a necklace of duckbills as long as his.

Liok's brother Bei, the sixth son of White Partridge, and a year older than Liok, had been initiated into the circle of hunters last spring. Soon all the boys Liok's age would undergo the initiation rites. Every boy, from his earliest years, dreamed about this event, the most important in his life. But Liok was the seventh son of a woman who had never given birth to a daughter, and by the laws of ancient belief, the father of a seventh son was thought to be a spirit—and from his earliest day Liok was taught that he must be, not a hunter, but, someday, a shaman. Last year, the old shaman had not returned from the hunts at sea, and now the hunters called for a new shaman. For this reason they had begun asking him, often and persistently, if he had had dreams at night, if he had spoken with the spirits. And in fact the worried Liok had begun to have terrifying dreams.

Spring came. The days lengthened and the sun became warmer. The snow began to melt even beneath the spruce trees in the forest, though during the night it would acquire a thin covering of ice. The deer and the elk were uncatchable; for the terrible hunger which had begun a month ago had left the hunters weak and sickly, and as in the previous year at this time, the hunters returned day after day empty-handed.

"We have no luck," they whispered among themselves. "There is no one to plead with the spirits for us. Kremen is to blame for the death of the shaman."

The men shot angry glances at the Glavni, the chief hunter, Kremen, a broad-shouldered old man, powerful and strong in spite of his years.

Listening to the dissatisfied whisperings of the hunters, Kremen pulled at his gray beard with his left hand, which had been maimed by a bear when he was still a young man. "We do need a shaman," he thought. "But Liok is too young, too ignorant. The hunters will complain even more as they remember the old shaman." It occurred to him that the Spirit of the River should be given a gift. The hunters, too, started to think that the Spirit of the River would be pleased to receive a gift. A young girl should perhaps be thrown to the rapids, and if the Spirit of the River was pleased he might smile on the people and break up the ice on the river. Then the water would be covered with birds and filled with fish.

Rumors of this reached the High Koldunya, who had witnessed this sacrifice many times in her long life. Even now she could hear the cries of her younger sister as she plummeted into the crashing water, and that had been many winters ago. Whom would they choose this time? Would it be black-haired Raven, the prettiest of all the young women and the daughter of her daughter? Perhaps they would choose Bright Star, for she too was beautiful. But no! Fox Paw could not allow this to happen to any of the girls. Like a she-bear cornered by wolves in the forest, she knew what she must do.

Fox Paw painted her arms and face with ocher and went to meet the hunters. She climbed up a cliff that towered over the path on which the hunters would be returning from their fruitless hunt in the forest. She stood there leaning on her tall staff and waited. The spring wind blew through her gray hair and rattled the figurines made of bone and flint that hung from the ends of her braids. The old woman was cold. She stood motionless, staring into the edge of the darkening forest.

Finally a group of exhausted men emerged from the trees. In a loud singsong voice Fox Paw spoke to them, "Hunters, my spirits have told me that it is time to try the new shaman. Let his spirits send food by tomorrow."

Kremen looked guardedly into the old woman's hunger-wearied face. She did not lower her eyes. "My spirits have spoken," she repeated.

Kremen turned to the hunters and ordered that Liok be brought before him. It was not far to the village and they did not have long to wait. The hunters and the High Koldunya watched silently as the Glavni spoke, "You are the seventh son of a woman who has never borne daughters. A shaman you are, beyond doubt, and you must call on the power of your spirits. The people are hungry. Food must be found. Let this be the trial of your power. Speak kindly to your spirits, for only they will save you if you fail us."

The boy turned pale. He looked helplessly at the old man and whispered, "Where am I to find food, when you, the greatest of the hunters, can find none?"

Searching for help, Liok turned to the hunters. Perhaps they pitied him as he stood looking at them, his face barely covered with the softest fuzz. He bore no resemblance to the former shaman, a wizened, gloomy old man. But no one dared to say a word, and even his three older brothers were silent. Liok looked up at Fox Paw. The slight, sinister smile on the old woman's crooked mouth frightened him even more.

"Where am I to get food?" he asked the hunters.

"Ask the Friend, he is kind," answered Kremen. Someone handed Liok the shaman's throwing club, and the hunters shuffled off toward the village. Fox Paw, leaning on her staff, went too. The boy sat on the jutting cliff and lowered his head. Some water caught in a hollow in the cliff served as a mirror, and he looked at his pinched face with its sunken cheeks. "Ask the Friend, he is kind," Kremen had said. The mysterious Roko was called "the

Friend" by the hunters. From time immemorial, from generation to generation, the story of the hunchback was passed down.

> Once upon a time, Roko was a hunter in the village just as other men. But the animals, the birds, and the fish listened to his call as if they knew him. Single-handedly he could round up a herd of reindeer, and the village was never hungry. The hunters loved him as the comrades of a great hero will, but the women laughed at him because of his hunched back, and his chosen mate gave the warmth of her hearth to another.
>
> Hurt and angry, Roko left the village forever. No one knew where he lived, but it was said that he was with the "forest people"—the brown bears; he lives with them still. He remains a friend to the hunters, and in difficult times he sends game to them, and guides the aim of their spears and arrows.

"Roko!" whispered Liok desperately, "send me game. Have pity on me or they will kill me."

The boy was stretched out on the cliff, his face pressed against the cold granite. "What can I do? Where can I find food? What will become of me tomorrow?" he asked. He lay for a long time filled with fear and despair. Suddenly, right by his head he heard the flap of large wings. Without even opening his eyes, Liok recognized the sound. He pressed himself against the cliff. Sliding clumsily along the icy rock with its feet stretched out wide, a huge swan slowly folded its majestic wings.

Raising his head slightly, Liok saw the swan come to rest. Anxiously stretching its neck, it was carefully studying the unfrozen patches of water in the ice. The nearness of the roaring rapids was disturbing the bird. This was the scout, the bird that flew before the flock, to find a place of rest.

If the swans were flying, then spring had really come.

Soon other birds would arrive and there would be much game and no more hunger. But Liok was not thinking of that now.

His hand stretched out quietly to the throwing club that Kremen had given him. Clutching it tightly he crept quietly toward the bird. Already very close, he saw the bird spread its wings and begin to fly. He made his move and the throwing club caught the swan squarely across its thin neck. It fell heavily to the ground, and Liok broke its neck with his hands.

Not daring to believe his luck, Liok kept squeezing the swan's neck, feeling its warmth. He wanted to lift the bird but lacked the strength. Only then did he realize what an enviable catch he had made. For a long time he looked at the feathers that were turned to multicolored hues by the setting sun.

He wanted to call together his kinsmen as soon as possible, to brag about his unexpected luck. But how could he give away such a splendid catch? The old men would take it and he would probably only get to watch as the others ate it.

Liok was not a hunter and did not know the hunters' customs. He lay down across the bird's wing, which crunched under his weight, and pulled out a thin row of feathers on the bird's neck. Then he pressed his mouth to the already cooling skin. His sharp teeth pierced the skin and vein. Salty, warm blood poured into his mouth—so much of it that when Liok, worn out by the long starvation, tore himself away from the bird, he was drunk with satiety and couldn't stand on his feet. All he could think of was sleep. He curled up beside the swan and gave himself up to slumber.

Chapter 2

ON THIS LIGHT SPRING NIGHT, White Partridge could not fall asleep. She was sitting at her hearth, occasionally throwing a few more twigs on the fire, and each time the rising flames were reflected in her tear-stained cheeks. The mother was anxiously thinking about her son Liok. How could a boy find any kind of food when even Kremen—the best of the best hunters—could find nothing? Had not the old man covered himself with magic necklaces, with bears' tusks and claws, dried-up pieces of wolf's heart, skulls of otter and beaver? And even so nothing had helped. Where then would a boy, who had never even been out on a hunt, find food for the tribe?

White Partridge began her divination. She held before her some short wooden sticks and, having mixed them up between her palms, she quickly separated her hands and watched, with a vigilant eye, how and where the cherry stick, which represented the shaman, fell. Was the birch stick, which promised success, in an auspicious position? Where did the aspen, signifying a bitter fate, fall? What place did the pine, harbinger of protective spirits, occupy, and did it guard Liok from the threat to his life from the spruce, the tree of dark and evil spirits?

Scores of times the sticks flew apart, sometimes to the side of darkness, the west, sometimes to the side of light, the east; sometimes to the side of warmth, the south, sometimes to the cold north. Each time they fell a different way, and the woman could not discover what was to befall her son.

Then the mother decided on a desperate move. Mumbling an incantation she had learned from her aunt when still a girl, she plaited her hair into seven braids. At the end of each braid White Partridge plaited in figurines carved from a rowan tree: a swan, a loon, a duck—the sacred birds of female magic; and animals—the protectors of the Koldunya—the fox, the otter, and the beaver. But to the end of the middle braid, the thickest one, she attached a human figurine. Then the woman donned a ritual shawl made from the skins of young deer, and with blood from her scratched palm, she painted magical signs on her forehead, cheeks, and chin. Just as her aunt had done in preparation for the rites of the Koldunya. So long as her son had not proved the power of his magic, White Partridge was not allowed to plait her hair into seven braids nor adorn herself with magical figurines. But though White Partridge was a woman who put great faith in the old laws, she was also a woman of great determination and strength.

It was difficult to climb the steep slope of the Sacred Cliff. And it was frightening to go against the ways of the tribe. But her maternal love gave her strength, and White Partridge arrived on the flat edge of the cliff.

There beside the dead swan she saw her sleeping son. So overcome with weakness was she that her legs buckled under her and she fell to her knees. "My son is saved! My son is saved!" she whispered, and weeping with happiness she then added, "Beyond doubt he is a shaman." And it was unclear from her voice whether she was pleased by this or not.

White Partridge did not dare to waken him, for it was believed that in sleep the soul of a shaman was soaring in the far-off world of the spirits. Whispering an incantation, she fingered the seven braids that fell onto her shoulders. She, and no one else, was to be the High Koldunya after Fox Paw.

The rays of the sun had not yet pierced through the cold night and it would have been good to return to her dugout, to the warmth of the fire. But she would not leave her son.

Not only his mother worried about Liok's fate. Bei, the sixth son, also worried about his brother. He knew that by ancient law it was forbidden to spill the blood of a kinsman, but Kremen could push Liok into the waterfall, could tie him to a tree in the forest to be eaten by animals. . . . The sun had not yet risen when Bei arrived at the Sacred Cliff, where his brother had remained the evening before. There he saw Liok lying on the wing of the dead swan and their mother with her hair in the braids of a koldunya. "Has he left?" asked Bei in a whisper.

"Yes. His soul is visiting with the spirits," answered White Partridge just as softly. "Tell Kremen that the spirits have gifted Liok with a swan."

His mother's words seemed to give new energy to Bei. He ran lightly and speedily down the cliff. On his way to the village he met some women on their way to the river for water. He gave them the happy news of Liok's catch and rushed on to the Glavni's dugout.

Kremen was lying in a sleeping bag made of deerskins turned inside out. When Bei flung aside the curtain to the entrance of the dugout, Kremen was mumbling something in his sleep. He was dreaming of delicious, filling food—the soft, fat meat of salmon.

"The spirits have sent us the happiness of spring!" said Bei, in a tongue understood only by the hunters. His words meant "The spirits have sent us a swan."

The Glavni opened his eyes and looked at Bei with a murky gaze; the visions of his dreams had not yet left him.

"The Friend has gifted Liok with the great happiness of spring," shouted Bei again.

Kremen raised himself up on one elbow. "Are you saying that Liok got a swan?" asked the old man and, after a short silence, added, "Call together all our brothers. Tell them to bring their spears and bows. Liok will renew their strength."

Bei went joyfully to fulfill the Glavni's orders. He was proud that his younger brother, whom he had so recently protected in boyish fights, had now become the shaman. Going from one dugout to another he loudly shouted, "Hunters, Kremen is calling you together!"—and each time he couldn't help boasting about his brother's success.

When the hunters had gathered, Kremen came out of his dugout and together they walked to the rapids.

According to the custom, only the shaman and the koldunyii were allowed to step on the Sacred Cliff. The hunters were allowed to stand at the foot of the cliff, and a small neighboring island was set aside for the women and children. The latter were already milling about expectantly when the men neared the sacred place. The hunters crossed the seething torrents by walking on a birch log that had been flung across, and stood looking up at the cliff.

On the other side of the cliff, Fox Paw was ascending slowly, groaning, while her koldunyii trailed behind her. Having reached the top, Fox Paw leaned on her staff, looked at White Partridge, and noticed that her hair was plaited into seven braids and that the ends were hung with the symbols of a koldunya.

The old woman's face became distorted with rage. With a practiced gesture she loosened the leather thong which tied together her nine braids, and they spilled out on her shoulders. The first and the ninth braids, on the ends of which glistened bone-carved shapes of the sun and moon —symbols of the might of the High Koldunya—shook on her bony breast.

"It will not be soon that you may plait nine braids!" she hissed. "I will live longer yet."

"But your last teeth will fall out before I will lose my first," White Partridge answered softly. "You have already lost a great many."

Fox Paw tightened her lips even more firmly. During the hungry days she had gotten scurvy and her teeth had rattled and then fallen out. But how did White Partridge know this? When the last tooth fell out, the reign of the High Koldunya was over.

Fox Paw stretched out her hands and whispered something indistinct. White Partridge also raised her arms and began chanting to the very same sacred song. She knew it as well as Fox Paw.

Liok continued his sweet heavy sleep, and it was necessary to wait patiently until he awoke. The hungry people wearily shifted their weight from one leg to another. Finally Kremen could wait no longer. "White Partridge," he said, "the people are tired. Help us."

"His soul is now far, far away. . . . He is there." The woman pointed to the east, where Liok's face was turned. "Who would dare to disrupt his visit with the spirits?"

Knowing that Liok was usually a light sleeper, White

Partridge stood on her knees facing west, so as to be able to see her son better and, rocking back and forth, sang gently, "The people await you, the people await you."

The eyelids of the sleeping boy twitched and opened slightly. Without raising his head from the rock, he noted the fluffy heap of swan feathers, the concerned face of his mother, her koldunya's braids, and the crowd of hunters standing in the distance.

"What is your command to the people? We want to know," shouted his mother. And the koldunyii obediently took up the chant, "We want to know. We want to know. We want to know."

Liok understood that he must say something without delay, give some kind of order. Now he was the shaman, and they would attend to his every word. His mother watched him carefully and asked, "Will the feathers of the swan bring luck to the hunters?"

Liok listened carefully to his mother's questions. "When we cook the swan . . . who will get the meat?"

It was not difficult for Liok to understand what was wanted. He must command each hunter to fasten a feather from the swan to his arrow, so that the spirit of the dead swan, longing for the company of its feathered companions, would guide the arrows to a flock of swans. To whom should he give the meat? He did not agonize long over this decision. Of course, it should go to the koldunyii. His mother was now one of them and she would get a share.

"When will you make your fire in the dugout of the shaman?" sang White Partridge, trying to direct her son in his new and difficult task. "The people have tired waiting for you. Return to us quickly!" she warned.

Liok arose. White Partridge joined the koldunyii and stood next to the High Koldunya. Liok was frightened.

Childishly, he squinted his eyes. Looking at him were old Kremen, the koldunyii, the hunters, his contemporaries—all waiting to hear what he would say.

"Hunters," began Liok, "attach the feathers of the swan to your arrows, they will lead you to your prey. The swan should be cooked and the meat given to the koldunyii."

The hunters frowned. Even though the portions of meat would be small, they would have welcomed them.

"Who will divide up the feathers?" asked Fox Paw.

"The Glavni will divide the feathers," answered the boy in a clear voice and, glancing at his mother, he understood that he had made the right decision.

Kremen angrily plucked the feathers from the swan and handed the hunters large feathers from the wings and tail. Then he skillfully carved the bird into pieces without breaking a bone.

"If Liok had been a hunter," the unhappy hunters whispered among themselves, "he would have known to whom he should have given the meat."

In the meantime the people had made a huge fire near the cliff. Soon water boiled in three enormous cauldrons and everyone, grownups and children, received some of the broth.

"Liok is a wise shaman," said the koldunyii as, to the envy of the onlookers, they hurriedly swallowed the cooked pieces of swan meat.

Chapter 3

THE SHAMAN'S DUGOUT stood apart from the main village and away too from the hunters' camp, where the men spent the summer months. At the village, the koldunyii were in charge and they jealously guarded their power and their secrets. Only hunters were allowed within the confines of the hunters' camp, and the shaman was not a hunter. The hunters too had their secrets which they disclosed only to the initiated.

The shaman was obliged to obtain from the spirits plentiful game for the hunters and to protect his people from sickness, pestilence, and hunger with incantations and invocations. He was to befriend the spirits so that they would in turn forewarn him of dangers to his people—invasions from unfriendly tribes, storms, and the like.

The shaman was taken along only on important hunts, so that his spirits would bring luck and safety. During the lesser hunts, the hunters themselves performed simple rites. The shaman stayed behind in his dugout.

Frightening rumors circulated about the shaman's dugout, into which not one among his kinsmen dared to step. Stories were told about how flaming spirits from heaven flew into it. These were perhaps ordinary falling stars, actually extinguished long before they reached the earth, but to the women in the village it seemed that they disappeared into the shaman's dugout. During the long winter night when the wind howled around the sleeping village, people thought they could hear voices from the shaman's dugout. "It must be the shaman," they thought, "talking with Roko, Friend of the Hunters." Many, many strange tales were told about this dugout hidden in the cliffs, surrounded on all sides by huge spruces.

Thus Liok approached his new and mysterious dwelling with some apprehension. Until this day he had, along with his kinsmen, gone out of his way to pass it by, and now he had to live in it. If he became ill—no one would come to see him, to find out how he was. If he died—he would just stay there. The new shaman would close up the entrance with branches and dirt and build himself a new dwelling nearby, in a spot just as isolated. But only one shaman, many winters ago, had died by his own hearth. All the others had died away from home.

Liok looked at his dugout fearfully. The storms had piled up a huge snowdrift at its opening. It took a good deal of work to dig through the snow pile and to bend back a small piece of the skin that firmly covered the entrance. From the inside came the sharp odor of wild onions. This encouraged Liok, and he decided to step into the semidarkness of the dwelling.

At first glance, everything was the same as in other dwellings. In the center were the blackened sooty stones of the hearth, and beyond it on two small boulders stood a hollowed-out log with a heap of deerskins on it. Apparently the old shaman liked to sleep warmly. Rows of clay pots lined an entire wall. Liok's predecessor had left his dwelling for the last time in the autumn while winter supplies were being stored up. What could be in those pots? Liok started lifting the covers one by one. One of them contained something light colored. Liok poked it with his finger—lard! Another held onions. And a third one—pieces of smoked venison!

All this food, which until yesterday could have come to him only in his dreams, now belonged to him alone. Biting into the frozen bitter-sweet pulp of an onion, Liok greedily picked over the dark brown pieces of venison, searching out those pieces on which the yellowish layer of fat was the thickest. He tore furiously with his teeth at the fibers of the hardened meat, looking around at the same time. Suddenly he backed off quickly toward the entrance. A frightful monster peered at him through the semidarkness. Shaking, Liok continued to retreat until his shoulder lifted up the covering of the doorway. A ray of daylight pierced through the opening and illuminated the wall. Liok took a deep breath. There was no monster. Drawn on a deerskin in charcoal and ocher was Roko, Friend of the Hunters. Liok recognized him by his humped back. Here and there a few holes showed through on the drawing and a dart stuck in his shoulder. The youth gasped in horror. The old shaman had dared to raise a hand against the Friend, had dared to bring him pain.

Hadn't Roko sent the swan during the night and saved Liok from death? The boy quickly removed the dart from the shoulder of his protector. "May your wound heal quickly," he whispered, smoothing out the torn edges of the hole. "You sent me a swan, and I will never bring you pain."

Having said this to Roko, Liok decided that their friendship had been set right.

A fire in the hearth would warm up the dugout, which had stood frozen through the long cold winter. Searching out the fire board and stick by the hearth, he filled the hole in the board with dry grass and began quickly to twirl the stick in it. The grass began to smoke as he worked, and finally a tiny tongue of blue flame appeared.

Soon thick billows of bitter smoke rose from the hearth. Liok pulled aside the fur covering of the dugout and flung it back. Then squatting down by the hearth, he lowered his head to the ground. The whitish smoke rose to the ceiling.

When the stones of the hearth were red hot, Liok stopped adding twigs. The last of the smoke floated out and it became easier to breathe. His eyes stopped tearing. The boy lowered the fur curtain and fastened it firmly with a rock. Then by the light of the smoldering coals he examined his dwelling once more. Roko gazed at him from the eastern wall opposite the doorway, but Liok feared him no longer. The northern wall was hung with several layers of animal skins. The boy carefully lifted the elk skin hanging on top. A large elk with antlers was portrayed in charcoal on the other side. Underneath the elk skin was a deerskin, upon which was drawn the image of a deer. And the wolf and lynx skins held images of their former owners. The only skin missing was a bearskin. But just nearby in a basket fashioned of twigs, Liok found a bear skull and underneath it two sets of dried claws.

Thus some of the simple magic of his predecessors was revealed to the young shaman. Without leaving the dugout, they had practiced their magic on the images of the animals that their kinsmen had intended to hunt. From now on Liok was to live the same lonely life—he must keep away from everyone and never enter dugouts where women lived. It was said that the mistresses of the hills and woods and rivers were very jealous. They would never forgive a shaman if he went to an ordinary woman. He must be friends only with them or the other spirits, the male spirits. What were these spirits like? Liok couldn't even begin to imagine.

For White Partridge, this day was unlike any other in her memory. Returning from the Sacred Cliff she passed through the village. On the very outskirts of it there was a tiny dugout. It stood empty and abandoned all summer and winter, and smoke could be seen blowing out of it only on those days when the koldunyii were instructing a new koldunya. The initiate had to stay there until the new moon. The koldunyii took turns visiting her and teaching her the secrets they kept from all their kinsmen, especially the hunters—the art of healing the sick, charms, incantations, and invocations . . .

White Partridge shoveled the snow away from the entrance with her hands, pulled the covering aside, and peering in from the threshold checked to see if her predecessor had left enough firewood, if the water bowl was intact, if there was a sleeping bag. Then she returned to the village. She would enter this dugout wearing new clothes given to her by Fox Paw and carrying hot coals from the hearth of the High Koldunya.

"Here already!" muttered Fox Paw grimly when White Partridge entered her dugout. "I haven't even had a chance to start up the fire properly."

"I will wait," answered White Partridge obediently. Mumbling something under her breath, the High Koldunya took out of a birchwood chest all the apparel of a new koldunya. A shirt and trousers of softest deerskin, to which she would attach long stockings made of fur. Over this she would wear a sleeveless vest, with the fur turned inside, lavishly and colorfully painted on the outside.

"Hurry, hurry, undress!" exclaimed Fox Paw. White

Partridge looked around. The entranceway was not covered and a ray of sunshine was peeping in.

"How can a woman show her body to the sun?" answered White Partridge, not giving in to the craftiness of the other. "If I go against the custom, you will be the first to banish me."

"So you want to be the High Koldunya?" said Fox Paw, no longer hiding her hatred.

"It was predicted by Clear Eyes, my mother's sister," said White Partridge without lowering her eyes. "This is remembered by all the koldunyii."

The aspen twigs that Fox Paw was about to feed into the sacred fire shook in her hands. Clear Eyes had been the High Koldunya before Fox Paw. Before her death she had predicted that Fox Paw would be succeeded by a woman bearing the name of a bird. But Fox Paw would not step aside easily.

"Not soon, not soon, will this be," she screamed. "You will not see my death."

The fire flamed up. Both women sat down on their haunches. It was hot, but there was a frosty draft by their feet from the opened entranceway. White Partridge and Fox Paw were silent. Time passed slowly. Finally the brushwood flamed up for the last time and the orange coals fell apart.

Then at a sign from Fox Paw, White Partridge let down the fur curtain. The dugout was bathed in a reddish glow, as White Partridge disrobed and looked at the old woman. During the ritual of dressing, the High Koldunya was to call the spirits to witness.

Fox Paw, however, was silent. Perhaps she hoped that White Partridge would not dare to touch the sacred garments without her incantations. But the old woman was mistaken. White Partridge knew all the sacred oaths.

Loudly proclaiming word after word, White Partridge undressed. Not waiting to hear the order from Fox Paw she flung herself forward on her outstretched arms and bent over the barely smoldering hearth. She invoked the fire to cleanse and purify her body of all diseases, to protect her from wicked charms and unfriendly spirits, and to make her as invincible as the fire itself, whose strength caused even rocks to crack.

The High Koldunya watched Liok's mother with fear and hatred. Fox Paw's power was great. No woman of the village dared to disobey her. Even the hunters feared the High Koldunya, and Kremen himself dared not contradict her. She glared angrily at White Partridge, who was still strong and healthy while she, Fox Paw, became feebler with each spring. When her weakening arms could no longer lift the heavy staff, the mother of the new shaman would take her place at the sacred rituals.

"Woe is me, woe is me!" thought Fox Paw listening to the ancient words echoing in the dugout. . . .

Having finished with the invocations to the fire, White Partridge straightened up. "You must speak!" she commanded the old woman. "I know all the words."

And Fox Paw had to call on the spirits to endow her rival with strength as she helped her dress in the sacred costume. The instant the old woman faltered or missed a word, White Partridge supplied it.

"How dared Clear Eyes teach you the words of the koldunyii," said Fox Paw angrily when White Partridge had finished dressing herself. "You were just a child then."

"The spirits instructed her. They told her I would be a High Koldunya," answered White Partridge. "Give me the coals."

"Prepare yourself, prepare yourself," whispered Fox Paw, and looked at White Partridge with such malice that her heart froze. "Just remember this. You will never plait your hair into nine braids! You will never see my grave, but I will laugh over yours yet!"

The initiate had to carry the hot coals with her bare hands. This was one of the trials that had to be undergone by the woman who wanted to light a fire in the dugout of the koldunyii. Fox Paw purposely picked out coals that were still smoking with blue fire.

Tossing them up in the air and from hand to hand, White Partridge ran to the dugout at the edge of the village. She threw the coals in the hearth, surrounded them with dry grass, and blew them into flames. Screwing her face up in pain from her burned palms, she slowly added kindling, watching carefully that an aspen twig was always burning. Disturbing thoughts overwhelmed her. White Partridge believed, like all the other women of the settlement, that the High Koldunya could foretell the future of all of them. Fox Paw had said, "You will not see my death." That meant that she, White Partridge, would die before the frail old hag. And if she didn't die from a natural death, the High Koldunya would try to send disaster her way.

It was the custom that the new Koldunya stay awake for three days and three nights. The longer she did not give in to her need for sleep, the stronger would be her powers. White Partridge's aunt, Clear Eyes, had spent five days and five nights without sleep, as had Fox Paw. When they finally slept, they fell into such a deep sleep that nothing could have awakened them. Then people said that the sleeping woman's soul was visiting with the spirits. Some women went into a frenzy from lack of sleep. They became delirious and screamed and threw themselves about. Then their kinsmen whispered that the spirits had come to visit with her. When this happened to a koldunya, she was considered to have even greater powers.

"The High Koldunya is very cunning," thought White Partridge, watching all the while that her fire did not go out, "what if she thinks up some mischief for me while my soul is visiting with the spirits?"

This was an unhappy time for Liok as well. He was warm, and he had enough to eat, but his fear of the new life he was leading never left him. For the first time he sat before a hearth that was not his mother's.

"What is she doing now?" he thought sadly. "It would be good to take her some food."

He filled a pot with meat and onions and left his dugout, carefully fastening the bottom of the fur covering in order to keep the warmth from escaping.

It was barely evening, but the village was very quiet. The dugouts were covered to their very tops with the snow of winter storms, and they looked just like snowdrifts. If the snow around them had not been so tramped down and strewn with debris, no one would have thought that people lived there. The village that in the summer was so lively and noisy seemed quite dead now. From one dugout only came the sobbing cry of a child. It disturbed no one, this weak and pitiful cry, and Liok thought, "It will probably die tonight."

Unnoticed, Liok made his way to the dugout of his mother, raised the door covering, and stopped. There was no one in the dugout; only cold ashes lay on the stones of the hearth. Only then did he realize that enormous changes had also taken place in his mother's life. Now she was the mother of a shaman, and herself a koldunya. She would not be found here in the dugout of his childhood, but rather in the dugout of the koldunyii on the outskirts of the village.

White Partridge was sorting out in her mind the incantations taught to her by her aunt to protect her against danger, when she saw the fur curtain move. She jumped—had Fox Paw already sent spirits to harm her? But it was only Liok standing on the threshold. "Don't come in, don't come in," she cried. Liok stepped back in fear. She ran out of the dugout and firmly closed the entrance behind her. "No man dares to cross the threshold of this dwelling. A shaman is not even allowed near it."

"I brought you such good food, and you chase me away," said Liok sadly.

"Now you are a shaman yourself, and you are not allowed to come to me. Don't you know that your spirits are enemies to us, the koldunyii?"

Such sadness was written all over Liok's face that the mother's love overcame her fear.

"The spirits sent you a swan to prove that you are a real shaman. You are my seventh son, and I have borne no daughters," White Partridge told him proudly. "From the summer that you were born, I have allowed no hunter a place by my hearth. I had faith that my Liok would be a great shaman."

Liok's head drooped lower and lower, and he seemed so hurt and helpless that the woman could not repress the pity she felt for her youngest son.

"Let us go to the Sacred Cliff," she said, looking around at the snow-covered dugouts. "There at least people will not see us."

Even Liok's gift, the pot filled with food, she dared not take into her dugout and, hurriedly shoving a piece of meat in her mouth, she buried the pot in the snow by the doorway.

At the place on the cliff where the night before the dead swan lay, now sat a raven. The raven was patiently pecking at the dried blood of the swan that remained on the stones. Seeing the people, he bent his head to one side, and, as if to threaten them, opened his beak.

"Very bad, oh, how very bad!" said White Partridge becoming quite pale. "The raven is guarding this place. See how angrily he looks at us?"

They went into a narrow cleft in the rocks, where the wind could not reach them, and Liok put his head on his mother's breast.

"A shaman is not allowed to touch a woman," whispered White Partridge with fear in her voice. Still, her hand found its way to his shoulder, as it had done in the past. They remained silent for a few minutes, and then the mother, as if in response to her own thoughts, quietly said, "The raven has not flown away, but he opened his beak. That is very bad."

"He was pecking at the dried blood and became angry when we disturbed him," said Liok, trying to calm her. The woman shook her head.

"You know, Liok, we are sitting together for the last time. You are a shaman, and I am now a koldunya. Soon I will meet with the spirits, and they . . ."

"What do they look like?"

"I have never seen them. But when you return today to your dugout, make them show themselves to you. . . ."

"How do I do that?"

"I can't say. The shamans of the neighboring villages once knew these things, but they were all devoured by hungry Khoro, who wears bloody clothes. In that time, our men had killed a hunter from another tribe, and we, fearing the vengeance of his people, moved to a small island in the Big Lake. Bloody Khoro destroyed all our neighbors but did not find his way to us."

"Who then will teach me to be a shaman?"

"No one. Our last shaman had not time to teach you his secrets. Our neighbors to the north and the south died before you were born. Now the spirits themselves must teach you."

Flapping his ragged wings and hoarsely cawing, the raven slowly flew over their heads.

"He wills me not to speak," shivered White Partridge. The sun went down, and the pink and violet snow instantly turned blue. The tops of the spruces became black and the sky turned a deep dark green. Somewhere up above, the first star sparkled. Then the snow turned an even gray, the cliffs darkened completely, and the many-fingered branches of the spruces seemed to become one with the cliffs.

Although White Partridge's hand still hurt her from the burns, she never stopped rubbing the barely whiskered cheek of her son. Liok tried many times to ask his mother what he should do when the hunters demanded that he practice his magic, but each time the hot palm of his mother tightly pressed his mouth shut.

"The raven willed us to be silent," whispered White Partridge. "He is sent by the spirits to watch people."

It became completely dark, and a cold dampness rose from the low places. White Partridge reluctantly rose to her feet.

"I must return to the dugout, or the fire will go out, and I cannot go back to Fox Paw for more coals. She will think that I fell asleep and allowed it to go out. Don't forget, little son, when you return to your dugout, ask the spirits to show themselves to you."

Liok did not get up. He was almost crying, so much did he want to stay.

"Well, for the last time . . . let us do as we did when you were little," said the mother and, pressing his face to her own, she slowly rubbed her cheek against his. This was the most tender expression of love that a mother could show.

When they neared the village, the mother said, "Do not come to me again. You are now the shaman."

Returning to her dugout, White Partridge began to blow at the dying embers of her fire. When the fire was blazing once more, she chewed slowly on the meat Liok had brought her and thought about her son.

In the old days if the shaman of a village died before he had had time to pass on his secrets to his successor, wise men came from the villages to the north and south and taught the new shaman all that they themselves knew. Now only the wind blew in and out of the deserted dugouts of their neighbors, and there was no one to instruct Liok. But the old hunters clung tightly to the ancient customs, and if Liok departed from the old traditions, they would have little faith in his powers. If there were even one misfortune in the village, people would blame everything on the new shaman. White Partridge tried to think of someone among the hunters who might instruct her son in the duties of the shaman.

And she had to worry about herself as well. White Partridge decided to make an offering to the spirits of the hearth, to invoke their protection. She cut off a piece from her fur robe, and asking the fire to accept this gift from her she placed it among the stones of the hearth. Smoke rose in a thin, unwavering stream, indicating that the fire spirit had accepted her gift.

"Will Fox Paw cause my ruin?" she asked, and laid a

new offering on the fire—a pinch of elk hair. The hairs started to smoke and a yellowish wisp of smoke again rose straight up in the air.

"There will be no misfortune," she sighed in relief. "Fox Paw will do me no harm."

Chapter 4

EXHAUSTED, Liok slept dreamlessly until morning under the pile of soft furs. Coals still smoldered under the ashes, and the boy fanned them into a blaze with little effort. Then he sat in front of the hearth with his back to Roko, a pot of smoked venison and a pot of lard at his feet. Only recently, he had dug through the snow around his dugout in a futile search for even a bare bone which might yet be boiled in a pot. Returning empty-handed, he had stared sadly at his mother's emaciated face, but his mother could only offer her son a thin bitter porridge made from spruce bark.

And now he had huge quantities of food at his disposal, but his happiness was spoiled by a worry he had never known before. His mother had said, "Make the spirits show themselves to you." But he did not have any idea how to entice them, how to speak to them.

Liok squinted at the hunchbacked Roko over his shoulder. The boy's shadow was falling on the deerskin that hung on the wall. When the coals in the hearth flamed up, the shadow wavered and it seemed as if Roko were moving his head from side to side. His arm was raised above his head, as if he were threatening Liok. The boy quickly turned away and moved closer to the warm fire, the kind protector of men.

Sometimes looking into the red-hot coals and sometimes closing his burning eyes, Liok thought about one thing only —what to do? Soon the hunters would gather for the big hunt. How could he help?

Who but Roko himself, Friend of the Hunters, could send them game? If only Kremen would ask *him* for help in the language of the hunters, the language known only to the initiated. Roko, himself a great hunter, would not deny his brothers aid.

But how could this be done? Kremen, like the other members of the village, was not to enter the dugout of the shaman. "Perhaps I should hang the deerskin with its image on the Sacred Cliff?" thought Liok, but he immediately remembered that nothing could be taken out of the dugout and then returned, for along with the object, the curses of shamans from faraway villages would also enter, borne on the wind.

Liok's thoughtful and distracted glance fell on a pile of river pebbles, lying under the hollowed-out log that served as the shaman's bed. Here were small stones and big ones, round ones and flat ones. Next to them were pieces of granite with sharpened edges. Liok wore around his neck a flat stone like these, on which was etched an intricate design that protected him from disease. When Liok had taken ill last winter, the shaman had removed the protective stone from his neck and had etched another design on the other side. Taking a piece of granite in his fist, he had held the sharp edge against the stone and hit it on the other end with a heavy stone. A whitish dot appeared on the flat surface of the stone, and the shaman barely moved the sharp granite and hit it again. Soon a double circle appeared on the stone. A circle, and especially a double circle, symbolized a strong protection. This way, the shaman had protected Liok from evil spirits and disease.

Remembering the shaman, Liok recalled something else, something he had completely forgotten. Not far from the village, in the heart of the forest, lay hidden a lake with a small island in the middle of it. A shallow stream joined this lake with the river Vig. Once it had been a big lake, but then it began to dry up, and slowly it turned into a swamp, overgrown with a rust red moss. The superstitious inhabitants of the village believed that this quagmire was the bloody mouth of the earth, which devoured man and beast alike—whoever dared to step foot on it. But Liok never believed these tales. Once in his childhood, while searching for birds' eggs, he was able to cross over to the island by hopping from stone to stone. There he found an enormous quantity of eggs, and he returned to the village happy and with a full stomach. From that time on, every year, in the spring when the birds laid their eggs, he stole off to this island.

There he had a favorite place—a cliff of red granite gently sloping off into the water. He often lay for long periods of time on this cliff, sunning himself like a lizard.

Once he went to the island in late summer, and as usual headed over to his favorite place. The water, which covered large portions of the cliff in the spring, was now asleep. Liok had shouted out in amazement—a drawing of a fish was exposed—white against the red granite. It was bent just like a salmon jumping over the rocks of the rapids. Liok bent over and touched the drawing of the fish with his fingers. The surface was rough from many tiny chisel marks.

The boy had been amazed—who could have made this drawing of a fish? He had not dared to ask anyone at the village. People who were banished from the village forever were brought to the island. No one else was allowed to go there.

Now, sitting in his dugout, everything came together—the drawing of the fish, the shaman who etched the design on the flat stone to protect Liok, and the drawing of Roko on the deerskin hanging in his dugout. Liok trembled in amazement at his realization: an unknown kinsman had undoubtedly lured salmon to that island with his drawing. He had performed magic! Liok would do the same thing, only better. He would chisel out the figure of Roko on the Sacred Cliff. Then the hunters themselves could ask their Friend for help.

And so, on the Sacred Cliff, where since olden times the koldunyii met to make their magic, was heard the even hammering of stone against stone. On the rock face appeared the head of Roko, then his big hump.

Liok stopped his hammering only to wipe the perspiration from his face. His hands were numb from fatigue but he continued to hammer out on the hard stone one little hole after another. Already the body appeared, and he was beginning on the feet. With each blow the figure of the Friend emerged more clearly, looking exactly like the one on the deerskin in his dugout. Roko was looking toward the river, which fed the village almost the whole year round.

When his hand became completely numb, Liok got up, and stepping back a few paces, tried to decide what kind of ears he should give to Roko—long ones, as the old men said, or short ones such as all people have.

Suddenly a cry pierced the air nearby.

"He has defiled the Sacred Cliff! Woe to us all! Woe to us!"

Fox Paw stood at the foot of the cliff amidst clumps of heather, shaking her arms in horror. On the shining surfaces of the stone gleamed the image of the hunchback so hateful to the women. How could they perform their ancient rituals when everything they did would be watched by Roko, patron of the men and sworn enemy of the women? Liok had forever robbed the women of their sacred place. Nothing worse could have happened.

Next to Fox Paw stood the other old women, and behind all of them stood White Partridge, whom they had brought to the cliff in order to instruct her in her new duties. The other women came running from the river below. They had been going for water when they heard Fox Paw's cry.

"Liok has defiled the Sacred Cliff! Liok has ruined us all!" wailed the chorus of koldunyii.

Liok's mother said nothing. The disaster seemed just as terrible to her as to the others. But what was done could not be changed, so only one thing was left—to quickly think of something that would save her son from misfortune.

"Death to you, destroyer!" shouted Fox Paw, and forgetting herself, she stepped toward Liok.

Now the boy himself became afraid for what he had done, but he knew well that it would turn out badly for him if his voice was not sure and his face calm.

"Do not come near!" he said loudly. "This is what my spirits have willed. Is it for you, woman, to speak against Roko, patron of the hunters!"

"We do not know Roko!" shouted Fox Paw. "Our spirits are stronger."

"If they are stronger, then let them chase the Friend from this cliff!"

The old woman was quiet. No matter how much she waved her arms, she could not erase the image that had been chiseled into stone.

"The shaman's spirits are enemies to ours, that is why they have willed Liok to take away our sacred place," said

White Partridge, finally deciding to step in on her son's behalf. "He cannot be blamed . . ."

Fox Paw quickly turned on White Partridge. "It is because of you that we have lost our sacred place!" she shouted and clawed her hooked fingers at White Partridge's face.

It seemed to White Partridge that the old woman wanted to claw her eyes out, and she stepped back in fear. Crouching like a cat before springing, the High Koldunya stepped toward her. One step, two, three . . .

The frightened woman stepped back again and again before the shrieking advances of Fox Paw.

"Mother!" shouted Liok, "the rapids!" White Partridge looked behind her, but it was too late. She had already lost her footing at the edge of the perilous cliff and without a sound she plummeted into the boiling torrent.

The faces of the people reflected the horror they felt. As Fox Paw straightened up, she did not feel the weight of her years, the chill of old age, for the death of her rival had gladdened her heart. She slowly turned to the crowd and raised her staff. "Our spirits have willed this. Our spirits have willed this. You saw how she herself went willingly to the Spirit of the River. He demanded a large gift . . . Now he will soon send us food."

The old woman started back to the village. Two others, her helpers, supported her under her elbows and carefully led her off.

The death of White Partridge had been so unexpected, had happened so quickly, that Liok and the women standing around did not come to their senses for a long time. Fox Paw had disappeared completely behind the riverside bushes and still no one else moved. Some were crying, some looked at Liok with pity, but no one dared say a word. Finally, the frightened and depressed women drifted home one by one.

Liok went nowhere. He stood for a long time without moving, looking straight ahead and seeing nothing. Later he collapsed to the rocky ground and covered his face with his hands. Above him, raising his hand high into the air, was Roko, Friend of the Hunters, whom the women feared and hated.

Fatigued to the point of exhaustion and again without any game, the hunters returned to the village. There they were greeted with incredible news—the young shaman had chiseled the image of Roko onto the Sacred Cliff and the Spirit of the River had taken for himself the shaman's mother. Worn out though he was, Kremen did not go to his dugout and did not send the hunters home. They all headed to the cliff and from a distance looked at the features of the hunchbacked Roko on the face of the cliff.

The Glavni shifted his gaze from the image of Roko to Liok sitting on the rock, his head in his hands. After long moments, Liok arose and looked at the hunters with eyes reddened from tears.

"My spirits have said this, 'As long as the hunters listen to the old women, they will receive no help from us!' " He spoke in a hollow voice that bore no resemblance to his usual boyish speech. "The spirits told me, 'Hammer out an image of the Friend on the cliff and let the Glavni himself ask for help.' "

Kremen was completely confused. What Liok proposed made Kremen's power even greater. But at the same time, he, not the shaman, would be responsible if the hunt did not go well.

No shaman had ever done this. Was this boy trying to trick him? The hunters did not know what to think either. Long ago they had all gotten used to the fact that the men hunted, and the shaman and the koldunyii bargained with the spirits on their behalf. Now, the hunchbacked Roko looked down on them from the cliff, and the shaman, in the name of his spirits, was inviting Kremen himself to enter into negotiations with the Friend of the Hunters.

Well, had any good come this year from the incantations of the koldunyii? Wouldn't it be better to listen to the young shaman and ask Roko for help themselves? Hadn't he sent Liok a swan just yesterday as proof of his friendship? The hunters remembered ancient stories of wonderful deeds done by the Friend, who did not forget his kinsmen. Shifting their weight from one leg to another, they contemplated the sparse words of their shaman. But no one dared to speak first. This was up to the Glavni. But the old man still could not decide how to react to this new decision from the spirits.

Liok again broke the heavy silence. "If the hunters will not again turn to the old women, then my spirits will let them make their own magic on the Sacred Cliff," said Liok slowly and loudly. "Come tomorrow at dawn to ask the Friend for his help at the hunt."

Kremen looked at the hunters standing behind him. "We will come to the cliff. We will ask the Friend for help!" they shouted. "Don't we make our own magic at the hunt?"

"Now go back to your dugouts," said Liok, raising his arm high above his head, "and when the sun has risen over the river, be here with your bows and arrows."

When a shaman raised his arm above his head, that meant that he was passing on the decision of his spirits, and the hunters had to obey him. Kremen looked at the boy glumly from beneath his bushy brows. But even he, the Glavni, could not argue with a shaman standing with his arm in the air. Lowering his head and frowning, the old man slowly turned around and went to the birch log lying across the rapids.

Kremen stopped in front of this slippery and unsure

bridge and stretched out his hand. The hunter walking just behind him took it and stretched out his hand to the one behind him. The third hunter did the same, as did the fourth and the fifth. . . . The live chain crossed the shaky log over bubbling waters.

Only Liok and three other hunters remained at the Sacred Cliff. These were his brothers and they had to perform the ritual of separation from their mother. Each one of them understood that the fast currents had carried their mother's body out to sea, but death had come to her at this spot, and this is where they had to bid her farewell.

At the foot of the cliff stood the oldest brothers. At a little distance from them—the sixth son, Bei. The youngest, seventh son of White Partridge, the shaman Liok, stood on the cliff itself.

Custom forbade them to cry or mourn the dead woman. They must be gay so that the dead would not want to leave the living.

"You are leaving us!" shouted White Partridge's oldest son as loudly as his voice permitted. "We will soon bring you good things to eat. Do you want some fat goose, or the soft breast of a duck?"

"We will not forget you," said the second son. "We remember how you cared for us."

"The first beaver I catch, I will throw into the rapids," promised Bei. "Tell the Spirit of the River to give it to you. You have always loved the meat of the beaver."

It was now Liok's turn. He knew that he must not cry, but his lips trembled and tears rolled down his cheeks. He fell on his knees and pressed his head against the cold granite of the cliff and whispered something. Even Bei, who stood closest to him, could not hear his words. The roar of the rapids muffled his brother's whisper.

When the four brothers had finally gone to their dugouts,

the Sacred Cliff did not stand empty long. Fox Paw soon reappeared. She came alone, without her usual companions, leaning on two long sticks.

Her sallow face was covered with perspiration, her dried-up hands shook, and her knees wobbled. Dragging her swollen feet, the old woman climbed the cliff with great difficulty. She stood in front of the image of Roko, and shoving the sticks under her armpits so as not to fall down, she stretched out her arms.

"Disappear!" she mumbled uncertainly, not moving her eyes from the hated hump glistening on the red cliff. "Disappear, I command you!"

Her breath came in short gasps, a cold sweat chilled her body. From time to time her eyes clouded, and the features of the hated Roko seemed to pale and swim before her. It seemed to her that with just a little more concentration the granite would again be as smooth and clean as it had been before this morning. Whispering incantations, the High Koldunya closed her eyes, but when she opened them, the fierce enemy was still there.

The failing old woman began to leave. Having taken three steps, she stopped and over her shoulder looked back once again in despair. Perhaps, now, he had disappeared? But the Friend of the Hunters looked down on her as before.

From that time on, the Sacred Cliff no longer belonged to the koldunyii. Never again would Fox Paw and her obedient women step foot on it. Their incantations, from time immemorial resounding from this cliff, would never again merge sounds with the roar of the rapids. And it was all the fault of a beardless boy! What kind of punishment could be inflicted on the defiler of the Sacred Cliff who had dared to take it from the koldunyii?

Chapter 5

OUT ON THE FROZEN WIDE EXPANSE of the bay, holes were cut through the ice two in a row, and thick straps were stretched from one to the other then tied to stakes frozen in the ice. The women from the village came to the bay early in the morning. They stood two by two at each pair of holes, one at the right stake and the other at the left stake. Untying the ends of the straps, they carefully pulled out from under the ice the seine—a wide rawhide strip to which were attached ten thongs with a bone hook on each.

Under the thick ice, schools of young cod swam slowly in the semidarkness. Many hooks were set out under the ice, but the catch was very meager—two or three large-headed fish to a seine were considered a good catch. More often than not, the tackle had to be lowered back into the ice without having removed even one fish. The women again tightly tied the ends of the straps to the stakes and wearily speculated about tomorrow's catch.

It was a long way from the village to the bay. During this period of hunger, not many women had the strength to get to the bay and back. The weakest ones stayed at the village with the old women and children. They sat on their haunches at the entrance of their dugout and, facing the sea hidden behind the forest, wearily waited to see what the fisher-women would catch that day.

The impatient children could not sit in one place. After a short time of waiting, they would run up the path leading to the bay, in order to find out more quickly from their mothers how much food they were bringing back. All too often, the entire catch would fit into the woven basket of just one woman. There was rarely a day when each dugout received a whole fish. During the months of plenty, the people would eat only the meaty back of the raw fish, and throw away the rest. But now they cut each fish into small pieces, and each family would cook their small piece in a clay pot until the fish—bones and all—resembled a porridge. Only then would they gulp down this murky chowder.

Each day usually began as the fisherwomen left for the bay and the hunters for the forest, but this day began differently. The hunters went quietly to the rapids instead of the hunt, and the women did not leave the village at all. During the night, an old woman, one of Fox Paw's assistants, had died. And a suckling infant's cry was silenced forever. And although death was by now a familiar visitor in the village, and all had become accustomed to it, it always called for a great deal of noise and fuss.

According to the custom, the dead koldunya would have been carried up to the Sacred Cliff, and leaned against the wall of the dead where the rituals of farewell would have been performed. Then she would have been buried by her dugout, where she had lived with her youngest daughter, Red Fox, and granddaughter, so that the koldunya even after her death could guard their peace.

But when the High Koldunya was told of the death of her helper, she was thrown into confusion, for Liok had defiled the Sacred Cliff and they could not perform the necessary rituals there.

Fox Paw's confusion was passed on to her helpers. Liok's name never left their lips. "Damned boy!" muttered Fox Paw, "you will yet be sorry that you have crossed me."

After much hesitation, the High Koldunya decided to perform the rites right there at the dugout. Work was found for everyone in the village—a grave had to be dug, and stones had to be collected to cover and make a mound over the body. This fell to the women and girls, while the koldunyii sat themselves around the body. Fox Paw placed the dead woman's head on her lap and placed her hands on the woman's shoulders.

"You must watch over Red Fox and protect her from harm," began Fox Paw in a singsong voice looking the dead woman in the eyes. "You must watch over Bright Star, your granddaughter." One after another the commands of the High Koldunya were repeated in chorus by the koldunyii. Fox Paw told the dead woman what messages to give the ancestors from the living relatives. When all the instructions and messages had been given, Fox Paw leaned down to the ear of the dead woman and whispered, "And also, don't forget to tell the spirits to punish the defiler of the Sacred Cliff. You know him, his name is Liok. Do not forget this."

The hunger-wearied old women did not have the strength to carry the dead woman in their arms, so placing her body on a deerskin they dragged it to the newly dug hole. They covered her body with dirt, and then everyone, from the oldest to the youngest, repeated the same words, "Do not go from us. Protect us," and they threw stones on the grave until a large mound grew over it.

The infant was buried without any ritual. The mother

carefully wrapped it in elk skin, carried it to the forest, and hung the bundle from a branch of a previously chosen birch tree. But although no one had shed a tear at the burial of the old woman, many tears were shed by the old tree.

Only after they had buried their dead did the women go off to sea. Today's catch was no better than yesterday's. Perhaps this night someone else would quietly go off to sleep and never awaken. Death from hunger was an easy death: it appeared quite unnoticed in the time of sleep.

Chapter 6

IT WAS NOT YET DAWN when Liok was sitting on the Sacred Cliff. It was a sad time for the young shaman, for now he was all alone. There was no one to advise him, no one to tell about the ancient beliefs, though his mother had known many of them.

Today, at sunrise, the hunters would gather at the Sacred Cliff to ask the spirits for success in their hunt. Liok himself needed success perhaps even more urgently than the others, for if the hunters returned today without any game, Fox Paw would say that Liok had angered the spirits by defiling the Sacred Cliff. But what could he do to make sure the hunters were successful?

Suddenly from somewhere up above he heard a vague familiar sound. Liok raised his head. He could see nothing in the dark sky, but he heard the sound again. There was no doubt about it—geese were flying. Liok laughed out loud. In order to attract salmon—one made an image of a salmon, and in order to attract geese—he would make an image of a goose. He had to hurry before the sun rose.

At the appointed time, the hunters, along with a frowning

and worried Kremen, came to the island at the foot of the cliff. They were astonished to see that on the cliff, alongside the figure of Roko, there now appeared a big, thick-billed long-necked goose. Liok pointed to the new image with his club and said, "Let each hunter throw my club at this goose. He who hits it now, will not miss during the hunt."

Liok handed his club to a young hunter standing on the side. This was Au, who several winters ago had taught little Liok how to hunt for molting ducks. But the club should have gone first to Kremen, the Glavni of the hunters.

The murmur that ran through the crowd, and the angry cry of the insulted old man confused the inexperienced shaman. But Au did nothing to rectify Liok's mistake.

"Since the shaman gave it to me, then that's how it must be!" he said loudly, waving the club. The Glavni grabbed the club away from Au. "Kremen still has his strength," he said threateningly, "Perhaps you would like to wrestle with me?"

Au stood silently, his head lowered. He knew well what terrible hands the old man had—once he had a man in his grasp, that man was as good as dead, save by Kremen's mercy.

"You will throw last!" ordered Kremen, and cocking his arm back far behind him, he threw the club. It whistled through the air and hit the goose on the cliff squarely in the neck. The old man looked up haughtily at the crowd around him. Sureness of hand was considered the most important quality in a hunter. He passed the club to old Niuk standing beside him. First the older hunters and then going down in age, they all threw the club at the image on the cliff.

"If you hit the goose now, you will not miss on the hunt," Liok loudly told each hunter. These words, spoken by a shaman friendly with Roko, inspired in each hunter a feeling of confidence and success. This kind of magic seemed more credible to them than the incomprehensible mumblings of the old women. As ordered by Kremen, Au was last to throw the club. The young hunter was so humiliated by this turn of events that he hit the mark neither the first nor the second time.

"Now go!" commanded Liok loudly. "On the small lakes between the cliffs you will find game."

Everyone left, and only Liok and Kremen remained on the cliff above the rapids. The young man was afraid. "You must also go," he said quietly, "your catch will be the greatest of all."

"I have seen many shamans come and go in my time," said Kremen not listening to him. "You are the first to go against our customs."

"My spirits have willed me to do as I did," answered the boy uncertainly. "How could I go against them?"

The Glavni took him by the arm and led him to the very edge of the cliff, beneath which, squeezed into a narrow bed of granite, rushed the boiling water of the rapids.

"Five winters ago I tossed a shaman from here who had dared to go against my will," said Kremen, not taking his eyes off the paling boy. "His spirits did not help him, and they did not harm me. And your spirits will not help you." Liok struggled in the old man's grip, but could not budge.

"I have done nothing bad to you."

"Done nothing? You have disrupted all the old order. You have chased the koldunyii from the Sacred Cliff and now they are angry with me. You want to put the blame for bad hunts on me. And today you have introduced a new ritual! . . ." Kremen squeezed Liok's arm so hard that he screamed. "Remember, if you do not wish to bring harm to yourself, we will live now, the way we lived before!" The old man leaned so close to the boy that his beard touched

Liok's face. "If you want to stay among the living you had better consult with me about everything."

Suddenly Liok felt himself being lifted above the ground. Everything darkened around him, and the roar of the rapids became closer and louder. He remembered the flash of Kremen's eyes, and then nothing.

When Liok regained consciousness, the old man was no longer on the cliff. The boy got up and moaned. There was a sharp pain in his shoulders. No sooner had the hunters left the cliff than Fox Paw had known everything that had happened. The young upstart had instituted a new ritual—the hunters had performed their own magic on the Sacred Cliff that had previously been the sole domain of the koldunyii. "If the hunters no longer believe in our spirits, what will happen to us? If they no longer listen to our wisdom, perhaps they will no longer want to feed us in our old age either," the old woman thought bitterly.

But the High Koldunya would not let go of her power so easily. She decided to have a talk with Kremen. Going out on the path that led to the Sacred Cliff to the forest, Fox Paw leaned on her long staff and waited for him. In a few minutes Kremen appeared.

"It was not my fault," said the old man as soon as he saw her, "You deal with the boy yourself." He wanted to pass her but she stood in his path.

"Is the shaman more powerful than the Glavni?" she asked.

"How could I have known what he was up to?" said Kremen, grimly looking at her. "The hunters believe in him."

"What will happen if wet-eared pups start going against the customs of the old people?"

"Right now he is lying unconscious on the cliff. He has learned a good deal just now. Perhaps he will be a little wiser," said Kremen evasively and, stepping over the staff that barred his path, he walked on. Then he turned around, "We are the same age. Was not your youth my youth as well? An insult to your old age is an insult to mine."

The old woman stood for a long time looking after him, until he disappeared completely in the thicket of spruces. Then she shuffled off to the village.

Liok, returning to his dugout, saw the High Koldunya walking along the path from a distance. Not wanting to meet up with her, he hid behind a clump of bushes. Barely placing one foot before the other, the old woman limped slowly past him, and Liok heard her muttering to herself, "I am wise and he is stupider than a young buck. I dealt with his mother and I will deal with him."

As soon as the old woman was out of sight, Liok stepped out on the path and with a sharp stone dug up the ground on which she had left a footprint. This was a sure way to bring destruction to an enemy. "You are wise, but I am more cunning than you," he whispered to himself.

Chapter 7

SPARK LOWERED her tired arms and, with difficulty, straightened her aching back. It was not easy for a starving woman to scrape animal skins clean and then to rub them until they were soft. Having rested a short while, Spark renewed her efforts, and, at length, the job was nearly done. She stood up and carefully looked over the skin, trying to decide what she would make with it. She desperately wanted to make something for her hunter, but only one animal skin was not enough. Better to make something for little Kao.

The young woman carefully put away the scraping stone, and from a leather pouch which hung from her belt she removed a stone knife, sharpened on one side. Placing the knife by her side, she looked over the skin one more time before beginning to cut it.

Just then the curtained doorway opened and Kao, Spark's pride and joy, slipped into the dugout. Seeing her youngster, the mother pushed the skin aside, fur side up, into a pile. Kao, the five-year-old hunter, looked at it and saw a big hungry wolf (wasn't everyone hungry in the spring?) ready to pounce on his mother. He ran to the corner of the dugout where his small bow and arrows hung. Spark smiled and stepped aside, and Kao, falling down on one knee just like a real hunter, drew his bow. The arrow whizzed across the room, tangling itself in the thick wolfskin. The boy looked proudly at his mother, then walked over to his kill. He had to retrieve his arrow, for he did not have many of them. Reaching out for the arrow, he quickly drew his hand back—what if the wolf was only pretending to be dead? He carefully looked it over, but the skin was lying still, and with a sigh of relief he took his arrow. Only then did Kao remember why he had come home. Once more only a small boy, he whined, "I'm hungry. Give me something to eat." Spark silently lifted the pot from the hot coals and set it before him. Sitting down on his haunches the boy tasted what was in the pot. He took three gulps and wailed, "It's bitter, too bitter." Spark knew very well that no matter how long the pine bark was boiled, it never lost its bitterness. But still, it was some kind of food.

The boy cried for a while and then quieted down. Sniffing softly he drew closer to the hearth and fell asleep. Spark laid more kindling on the fire and began to cut a jerkin for Kao from the twice-killed wolfskin. She placed the skin fur side down on a flat stone, and pressing down hard on the knife, she rubbed it slowly back and forth in one spot until the skin was cut. Then patiently moving the knife, she separated the unwanted parts from the future garment. Then she was ready to begin sewing. She took an awl, a bone needle, and a roll of strong pliable deer sinews out of her pouch. With the sharp awl, made from a chipped elk rib, she made a row of holes along one side of the skin. Then she drew the sinew through the holes with the blunt bone needle, sewing the sides of the skin together.

The young woman was so engrossed in this tedious work that she did not notice when the curtained doorway lifted. Bending his head under the low ceiling, a broad-shouldered hunter entered the dugout. Only then did Spark turn around.

"Au!" she exclaimed joyously, and at the same time stifled a sigh. How could she feed a tired hunter with the bitter porridge in the pot? But Au immediately handed her the carcass of a huge goose. "I killed three," he told her proudly. "Two of them were taken to the storehouse, and this one I brought to you."

Spark's nimble fingers were already plucking the feathers off the fat goose. She had always known that Au was the best of the hunters. As if in answer to her thoughts, the young hunter said, "But I was not the only one who returned with game. The new shaman has become fast friends with Roko. We made magic together with him at the Sacred Cliff this morning. And see the result." He nodded at the goose.

Spark, having plucked and cleaned the goose, placed it in the biggest pot she could find. "Liok is still a boy. Who would have guessed that he would turn out to be such a good shaman," she said thoughtfully.

"Roko loves the young shaman," said Au with conviction, "and how could he not love him? Had he not become a shaman, Liok would have made a wonderful hunter himself. Now that spring is coming, there will be more and more game, and Roko will chase it out to meet our spears and arrows."

The pot hanging over the fire began to boil. A delicious-smelling steam spread itself under the low roof. On the other side of the hearth, Kao tossed about in his sleep. He was dreaming that a wonderful-smelling piece of venison was running away from him and that he could not catch up with it. He leapt after it and woke himself in the process. Once again he experienced a wonderful aroma. Raising himself, the boy saw the goose cooking in the pot, and Au sitting next to his mother. He stretched out his little arms and laughed happily.

Chapter 8

THE LONG-AWAITED SPRING finally came. From high in the shining sky the trumpeting of cranes was heard, a sure sign that any day now untold numbers of birds would come flying. And in truth, toward evening one could hear from the ice-covered lakes the quacking of ducks and the loud honking of geese. With each passing hour newly arrived flocks kept landing on the large unfrozen patches of water in the midst of the ice. And, off by themselves, away from the noisy commotion, grand and silent swans swam by in pairs. The recently grim and barren lakes were hardly recognizable. Each piece of still-frozen ice and all the cliffs and shores were teeming with life.

The big goose chiseled on the Sacred Cliff was no longer alone, either. Next to it were a swan and three ducks. Each morning Liok made the hunters throw their clubs at the images on the cliff in order to insure a successful hunt. And since the hunts were very successful, no one doubted the usefulness of this new magic. Only Fox Paw shook her head. Hadn't there been just as much game last spring? But she did not dare say this aloud. Having suffered through a long famine, the people wanted to believe in the powers of the new shaman and in his strong friendship with the spirits. Overjoyed at the abundance of food, they sang the praise of the Friend of the Hunters, the kind hunchback, Roko.

During the early days of spring the hunters did not pass up any game that came their way, and the people ate even the tough meat of the loon. Later the hunters began to be more choosey. And wherever the hunters went, there was plenty of game.

At the village everyone worked without stopping. Goose meat spoils quickly, and the women and girls had to work day and night to get the meat cooked. No matter how much their hands and fingers hurt, no one rested. First the stiff, outer feathers had to be pulled out, then the fine down was carefully plucked. Then a long incision was made, and after the skin and underlayer of fat were removed, the goose was disemboweled. The insides, the neck, the head, and the feet were eaten the same day; everything else was preserved and laid in store. The meatiest part of the goose, the breast, was strung up with sinews and smoked over a fire. The skin and flesh were cut into small pieces and the rendered fat was saved in a bag made from the stomach of a deer.

In the winter when the smoked goose breasts cooking in the boiling pots gave off their delicious aroma, the people of the village would gratefully remember the noisy arrival of the spring birds. The more meat that was prepared and stored away in the spring, the less hungry the winter.

Once when Liok was coming to the village to renew his supplies of food, he met up with the young hunter Au. Au greeted him and said, "Yesterday, my brother Ziu heard that Fox Paw is planning to harm you. She has cast a spell on a piece of goose meat and has ordered my mother to give it to you when you come to her for supplies. What will you do?"

"My spirits will protect me," answered Liok confidently, though his voice wavered a bit. He did not have much faith in the protection of those whom he had never seen, neither awake nor in his dreams.

There were two women who kept the food and dispensed provisions to the people of the village. Liok could have avoided Au's mother, thereby avoiding danger, but he decided not to. "She does not know that I am on to the plot," he thought on his way to her dugout, "so she is probably keeping that piece of meat separate from the rest."

Au's mother led Liok silently to the storeroom dugout, and he watched carefully as she filled his basket with pieces of meat. "It's not here," he thought to himself, watching her hands, "she will probably give me that piece last." Liok had guessed right. Having almost filled his basket, the old woman took a piece of meat that was hanging by itself, away from the rest. "This is such a fat piece," she said, "you don't even have to cook it."

Liok grabbed his basket out of her hands and hid it behind his back. "Take that piece to Fox Paw," he ordered. "My spirits forbid me to eat it."

"You are truly a great shaman," the dumbfounded woman whispered. Glancing fearfully at the shaman, she dragged herself off to the dugout of the High Koldunya.

The time had come when the adolescents of the village would wander about by the neighboring lakes and ponds in search of eggs. Although Liok was no longer considered a boy, and although egg hunting was not considered fit work for a shaman, his stores were low again and Liok was afraid to go to the village for more. Moreover, Liok preferred the taste of fresh eggs to that of the preserved goose meat. He made up his mind to go egg hunting.

Slipping off to the forest unobserved, he quickly found many eggs, and having eaten his fill, he began to gather more to take back to his dugout. Suddenly his keen ears caught the sound of something moving in the forest. Liok listened carefully. This was not an animal—a human being was approaching. He quickly hid himself in the bushes so as not to be seen by anyone from the village.

The approaching footsteps were very slow, and as Liok peered through the bushes he was not surprised to see Fox Paw limping along on the shadowy path. She was carrying something heavy, for she appeared to be bent over even more than usual, and when Liok was able to make out what it was, his astonishment was so great that he nearly revealed his presence. Fox Paw was carrying a child. Liok recognized the girl, Little Bird, she of the ringing, musical voice.

"Where could she be carrying the girl?" thought Liok, quietly following the old woman. The forest was thick and dark, but Fox Paw limped along till she came to the very darkest, most impenetrable part of the woods. Here the woman laid the sleeping child by a fallen log and, muttering something under her breath, turned back to the village alone.

When she was gone, Liok approached the little girl. He was overcome with pity for the sleeping child and anger for Fox Paw as he realized that a small child could never survive a night in this part of the forest. Liok picked her up and began to make his way back to the village, but as he walked, he thought to himself, "If I return Little Bird to her mother now, I will never know what was in Fox Paw's mind."

Then Liok remembered the hidden island where he had found the image of the fish chiseled in stone. "I will take her there," he decided. "There are no animals on the island, and there is plenty of food. She will be safe and I will see what happens." Through all this the child slept as if under a spell, and indeed, Liok thought, that must have been the case.

The little girl's disappearance was not noticed immediately. In the spring all the children fed themselves by gathering birds' eggs. They would often spend the night sleeping in small groups of four or five in the woods near to the village. But the next day, when the little girl had not returned, and her playmates had, the worried mother ran to the koldunyii for help. The old women began their magic, but could not discover the whereabouts of Little Bird. On the following day, Fox Paw declared that Liok was responsible for her disappearance.

The wind carried to the shaman's dugout the furious cries of the women. Hearing them, he painted his face with red ocher and went to the village to face them. The women met him with threats. "Why have you killed my daughter?" cried the girl's mother.

"Is your daughter dead?" asked Liok.

"You have killed her," Fox Paw interrupted. "My spirits have told me all about it."

"So that's what it is," thought Liok to himself. "In order to do away with me, that wicked old woman was ready to sacrifice an innocent child." Then raising his arms above his head, he spoke loudly to the women.

"You have heard," he began, "that Fox Paw's spirits say the girl is dead."

"Yes, yes," the old woman croaked hoarsely, "my spirits have spoken."

Liok turned to Little Bird's mother. "Fox Paw says your daughter is dead. My spirits know that she is alive. Which of us do you believe?"

The woman wavered. "My heart does not know whom to believe," she whispered, "I don't know."

"If you believe," said Liok quietly, "that she is still alive, then you will soon clasp her to your breast."

"I believe, I believe, I believe," sobbed the poor woman, "I believe that my daughter is still alive."

Liok sighed with relief. "Women!" he began again, "if

I fail to find the child alive, then let me be put to death. But if the child lives, then Fox Paw, who has lied to you, must die."

"Let it be so," said the women in chorus. The village had passed sentence. Now either Liok or Fox Paw was doomed to die.

In order to show the strength of his spirits, the young shaman put on a hat of lynx fur and began a twirling dance around Fox Paw. The High Koldunya became fearful; she did not know this kind of magic. Spinning about in place so as to keep a wary eye on Liok, she became dizzy and fell to the ground.

When the old woman came to her senses, the shaman ordered her and the girl's mother to follow him to the river where the three of them got into a canoe made from a hollowed-out aspen log.

The High Koldunya sat on the bottom of the canoe, hunched over and holding her head in her emaciated old hands. Her thoughts were confused and there was fear in her heart—for Liok's eyes were glistening with too much confidence.

Finally the canoe landed on the little island and the three of them stepped out on the shore. Liok, standing next to the mother, told her to call to her daughter.

The mother called, but there was no response. She called again, her voice faltering, but there was no answer. The High Koldunya's lifeless eyes began to light up. She stood a little straighter.

"Call louder," ordered the shaman, "my spirits are calling with you."

The mother called once more. Her cry seemed to linger in the still air, and she trembled. Fox Paw untied the thong that held back her nine braids.

"Do you hear?" she said triumphantly to Liok. "The spirits of the forest are laughing at you."

But Liok, jumping onto a rock, began calling himself, "Come to us, Little Bird. Your mother is calling you."

And suddenly some bushes in the distance parted, and the little girl came into view.

"My daughter, my daughter," cried the mother running to her child. Seeing the girl, Fox Paw began to tremble.

Liok helped the mother and her little girl into the canoe. Not a word was said, but it was understood that the High Koldunya was to be left behind to her death. Later this was understood by the entire village, for everyone saw the happy woman with her child safely returned. There would be no grieving for Fox Paw.

Chapter 9

EACH SPRING, from time immemorial, vast numbers of herring had invaded the bay. They gathered in the deep waters of the icy ocean, and in one huge school they swam into the bay, to spawn in the shallow offshore waters. Not far behind them were the salmon, feeding on the smaller herring, and fattening themselves for the exhausting run upriver.

For the people of the village, the run of the salmon was a most important event. Salmon was a staple in their diets and easily caught. The dried flesh of the fish fed the village for many winter months, and fresh, it was a favored delicacy. In previous years at this time the koldunyii would come to the Sacred Cliff to attract the salmon with their magic. But the Sacred Cliff was no longer their domain, and Fox Paw was gone. The new High Koldunya had neither the wisdom nor the cunning of her predecessor. And whether she was confused because there was no place from which to call the salmon, or because she wanted to avenge Fox Paw's death, she declared that this year there would be no run of salmon because of Liok.

Though there was now plenty of food, the terrible days

of hunger were still fresh in the minds of the people. The very thought that there might be no salmon made them panicky. "How will we live?" they shouted. "We will perish because of the shaman. Our children will perish."

Returning from the forest to his dugout, Liok heard the rumble of voices, first from far off, then closer and closer. He hid himself behind a tree and watched as a throng of women, all shouting and waving their arms, ran from the village to his dugout. Not daring to come too close, they stood at a distance, making threatening gestures with their fists and throwing rocks at the dugout.

Liok reached into the leather pouch that hung from his belt and, taking out a piece of ocher, painted his hands and face with it. Then, sneaking up to the hysterical women, he slipped unnoticed into the crowd. When one of the women saw the strangely painted face of the shaman who had seemingly appeared from nowhere, she began shrieking with fear. Then the others saw him, and in moments they had all scattered into the woods.

But just as Liok was entering his dugout, he saw Kremen approaching. Kremen too was worried about the High Koldunya's prediction. He came up to Liok and said bluntly, "The High Koldunya says there will be no salmon because of the shaman. What does the shaman say?"

Liok replied, "The mind of the Koldunya has wandered from her frail body. The salmon will come, as they have always come in the spring."

The women, who had regrouped by the edge of the clearing, now came forward again. "He lies," they shouted. "The salmon fear hunchbacked Roko on the cliff. Animals listen to the Friend, but he is no friend to fish."

"My spirits," said Liok, "are true friends of the village. There will be salmon," he shouted, and went into his dugout where he remained until all had gone home.

The village was worried and restless for several days. The hunters tended to believe the shaman, while the women trusted the High Koldunya—and the arguments were endless. Time passed slowly, and before very long everyone felt that the run should already have begun, and still the salmon did not come. The High Koldunya wore a secret smile on her face, and even the shaman started to worry.

One evening he left his dugout and headed to the sea. Reaching the shore of the bay he sat down in the moonlight and tried praying to the spirits of the salmon. When he was through praying, he cursed them, and when he was through cursing, he, the shaman of the village, cried himself to sleep.

When he awoke, Liok was confused and disoriented. He had not meant to spend the night, but as his keen eyes scanned the ocean, he knew that his good luck—his spirits—had not failed him. There, flying low over the water, pink in the light of the dawning day, was a huge flock of gulls. Even the youngsters of the village knew that the gulls followed the salmon just as the salmon followed the herring.

Now Liok was at peace. Returning to the village, he loudly announced to everyone, "My spirits are battling with those of the High Koldunya. The salmon will come soon." And, indeed, two fat salmon were found the next day, thrashing about on the rocky shore near the rapids.

Thus the long-awaited salmon catch began. The salmon were caught from rafts. While one man pushed the raft with a pole, two others beat the fish with clubs, then harpooned them out of the water and tossed them onto the shore. Boys, too young to fish, picked up one fish after another, piled them up in baskets, and dragged their heavy loads to the women. The women slit open the bellies of the fish, gathering the roe into large pots, and hung the fish on wooden poles to be smoked over large fires.

On the morning of the fourth day, there were noticeably fewer fish, and on the fifth day, only the scales glistening on the rocks along the shore remained.

A bright fire burned in the hearth of every dugout, for the village celebrated a double holiday—the end of the successful salmon catch, and the departure of the men for their hunters' camp, where they would remain until the end of the hunting season in the fall. The people feasted the whole day and night, and with the coming of the new sun the hunters left their dugouts for the camp.

As long as the salmon catch lasted, no one had time to think about the High Koldunya and her ill-fated prediction. The old woman had spent these days in her dugout, not daring to show her face, for she knew the fate that awaited her.

The women, having escorted their men as far as the edge of the forest, now gathered at the old woman's dugout. She emerged from behind the deerskin door, took one last look at the hearth that would never warm her old bones again, and closed the doorway behind her. The magical amulets no longer hung from her braids, and she no longer carried the sacred staff.

With no outward sign of sadness, she bowed to the women who watched her, then unhurriedly walked out of the village, accompanied by a few of the koldunyii. She walked straight ahead without looking back, and those who accompanied her fell back one by one until, at the edge of the forest, she was alone.

She was to walk, without stopping, to the west until her strength gave out, and the old woman carried out this cruel punishment to the letter.

Chapter 10

ON THE DAY after the hunters had moved into their summer camp, Bei came back to the village, though he stopped at the very outskirts, as was required by the old law. Cupping his hands to his mouth he shouted one name after another: Meku, Tibu, Ziu. . . . The boys whose names were called came running out of their dugouts with joy on their faces. They were called by the hunters for the rites of initiation.

In his lonely dugout Liok heard the names of his childhood playmates. Though he knew his name would not be among those called, he could not contain himself and ran to the place where Bei was standing. Coming close, but staying out of sight, he heard Bei instruct the boys on the nature of the preparations they must make for the evening's initiation.

Liok felt even more alone than when he had first entered the shaman's dugout. Though he had been told for as long as he could remember that he was someday to be shaman, he had never really believed it, and like every other boy, he had dreamed of the day when Kremen would hand him his bow and his spear. He knew better than all the others the habits of the birds and the ways to move in the forest without making a sound. The initiation was the most important event in the life of every male, and he, Liok, was to be deprived of that pleasure.

When the excited boys ran off to the village to brag about their news and to ready themselves for the evening, Liok approached his brother. Bei, a hunter, understood the cause of Liok's unhappiness. "I am sorry," he said, "but you help us in your own way. Without a shaman, who would speak for us to Roko, Friend of the Hunters?"

Liok only sighed. "How will they be initiated?" he asked.

"Why do you ask what it is forbidden for you to know?" Bei reproached him. "I don't ask you about your visits with Roko. Please, don't make it difficult for me."

Liok wanted to shout that he had never even once seen any of the spirits, but he dared not admit it, not even to his brother.

The brothers stood together in silence for a while longer, then Bei remembered that Kremen was waiting for him and he headed for the hunters' camp. Liok went into the village, passing the luckier young men who were talking excitedly together. When they saw the shaman, all save Meku, with whom Liok had constantly fought as a boy, fell silent. "When we go off to the hunt," taunted Meku, "you had better take good care of the infants, or the old women won't feed you."

Liok thought better of spending time in the village and hurried back to his dugout. He sat there the whole day, but toward evening he could stand it no longer and quietly stole off to the hunters' camp.

The camp was in the center of a large clearing. No trees overlooked its high walls, so that the initiation of the hunters would be a secret not only to the others in the village, but to the birds and small animals of the forest who could warn the other animals of the hunters' plans. Thus Liok was forced to climb a big fir tree at the edge of the clearing. From there he could see nothing, but he could hear the hollow, monotonous sound of the drumbeat as the ceremony of initiation began.

Liok heard voices raised in song, though the songs and even many of the words were unfamiliar to him. Then there was a long silence, pierced at last by a long, protracted scream. Liok thought it was a voice he recognized. No sooner had the scream subsided than angry voices were heard and the gates of the camp were opened. A naked boy stumbled out and fell to the ground. Kremen appeared and shouted, "Your place is with the women and children until you learn to withstand pain like a man." The gates slammed shut.

Liok recognized the shivering youth as Meku, who just that morning had laughed at him for not being a hunter. "I would never have shamed myself that way," Liok thought bitterly.

In a little while the drums sounded again and the music was so rhythmic and pounding that Liok wanted to jump and dance. Then the gates opened and the men came running out, faces covered with bark or bits of fur and leather. First were Kremen and Bei, with Tibu, naked and bloody, between them; behind them were the other initiates and the rest of the hunters. Shouting happily among themselves they ran right past the fir tree which concealed Liok and disappeared into the forest. Liok climbed down from the tree and quietly followed the hunters.

The hunters descended into a low gully where there was a stream. From behind the trunk of a fat tree, Liok saw that the initiates smeared themselves with thick clay and then washed themselves off in the stream. As he watched he began to shiver just imagining how cold they must be.

Then they began to put on their new clothes. Once dressed, they formed a line in front of Kremen, who handed each one a bow and a spear. Liok almost cried. Was he never to hold the smooth wood of a spear in his hands? Then suddenly Kremen gave an order, which Liok could not hear. The new hunters fell to the ground as if stalking prey, listening with their ears to the ground. Then they began moving toward the tree which hid Liok—almost as if they knew he was there. Liok knew that if he was seen there would be no mercy for him. He stepped back to move to another tree, and a dry branch cracked loudly under his foot. In panic, Liok turned and began to run.

"An animal, an animal!" shouted the hunters, and they took off after him.

A spear whistled past him. The footsteps came closer and closer. In desperation, Liok hid his face as best he could with a mask of leaves, and hunching himself over, stepped out from behind some bushes, shaking his fist at the hunters.

The hunters halted and the silence was broken by a half-frightened, half-joyful voice, "It's Roko!"

Liok unclenched his fists and waved his hands as if to say that they should stay away. The hunters remained frozen for a few minutes and finally, obediently, turned back.

Never before had Roko shown himself to the hunters, and the hunters took this as a very good sign—the hunt this year would be excellent.

Chapter 11

IT WAS TIME for making new pots. On a quiet warm day the women and girls gathered by the river. The girls had gathered a large heap of yellow clay, and the more experienced women were adding coarse white sand to it. On a flat boulder they crushed pieces of an amazing mineral, asbestos, which did not break into sharp pieces, but fell apart into fibers like a piece of rotted wood. These fibers were added to the clay, so that the pot became sturdy after it was fired and did not crack in the heat. Water was poured into the clay, and three older girls began to mix the viscous mass slowly with their bare feet.

Soon their jokes and laughter quieted down, and sweat began to pour down their faces. Mixing clay for pots was a difficult and tiresome task.

Suddenly Spark shouted, "Look at the helper we are getting! We will get some good work out of him." Everyone looked up and there was much laughter. Approaching them was an older woman dragging along a reluctant boy. His mother, ashamed to meet the eyes of the other women, was bringing Meku to make pots with the women as Kremen had ordered. He was to have the status of a woman until he could prove himself a man. The girls mixing the clay eagerly turned the tiresome job over to the embarrassed boy. Not daring to raise his eyes, Meku grimly began to knead the pasty clay with his feet, while the women, each trying to outdo the other, heaped scorn on him.

"Our Meku has made a turnaround," said one of the women; "just recently it seemed he was a man, and now he has turned into a woman."

"Where are your children, Meku?" asked another one. "Don't forget to suckle them."

Meku worked quietly, barely able to hold back his tears. But the taunts did not stop. "If you ever become a hunter," laughed Bright Star, "and you meet up with a terrible horned elk, just shout loudly and I will come to your aid."

Mixing the clay with sand, Meku silently cursed the mockers, and for the hundredth time promised himself that now he would gladly bear any pain, even if Kremen were to cut him up into tiny pieces, without uttering a sound.

The laugher and jokes of the women cut his mother's heart like a knife. She had brought four sons into the world. One of them had died in an uneven battle with a bear, two were out hunting with the other men, and only this one, her youngest, had brought shame on her gray head. Angrily, she pinched off a piece of clay and flattening it out in her palms threw it at her son. "Knead the clay more carefully, you miserable cur," she shouted, "you are not good for anything else."

Finally, when the clay glistened under Meku's feet, Spark said, "We can begin."

The women sat down in a semicircle. Each poured a pile of sand in front of her and next to it put a large piece of clay.

The modeling of the pots began, and though Meku was left with nothing to do, he could not leave without the permission of the eldest woman, whom all the younger people obeyed. Trying to avoid attention, he sat down behind his mother and began to watch as she fashioned pots out of the shapeless clay. She cut a small piece of clay from a larger mass, rolled it into a ball and pressed it with her thumb and then, smoothing it out with her palms, modeled the rounded bottom of the pot. She kept wetting her hands in another pot filled with water to keep the clay from sticking to them and to keep the surface of the pot smooth. Placing the clay onto a shallow pile of sand for support, she began to build up the sides of the pot. Rolling out a long clay strip, Meku's mother pressed it around the edge at the bottom. The clay strip was only long enough to go around one and a half times. A new strip was carefully pressed onto the end of the previous one and again wound around building up the walls of the pot. Winding strip after strip in this way, the walls slowly grew wider in the middle and then narrower again toward the top. Meku's mother pressed the inside and the outside of the pot with her wet hands to smooth out the places where the clay strips came together.

When she decided that the walls were high enough she pressed the edges of the top out to form a rim. Then she took a sharp pointed bone and began to carve designs on the sides. Meku gave out a snort. "I could do that better," he boasted. "Are you still here, you miserable coward?" The women were delighted to take a rest for a few minutes, and the jokes about Meku began again. Then Bright Star threw a piece of clay at him, and Magpie, not wishing to be outdone by her friend, neatly threw a piece that landed right on the boy's nose.

"What did Kremen tell you to do?" asked his mother sternly.

"To make pots," he mumbled indistinctly.

"Here, make them!"

While he had watched the women working, it had seemed quite easy. But now the clay was like a slippery eel in his clumsy hands, and the strips of clay, not wanting to stick together, kept sliding out of his grasp. Finally, he managed to stick one pot together, but it was such an ugly lopsided one that, while the women laughed until tears rolled down their cheeks, Spark took the wretched pot and dumped it on his head. Meku spent a long time at the river trying to wash the clay out of his hair.

When, almost crying, he returned to the women, the pots, having dried slightly in the wind, were already standing in the red-hot coals. The fires were carefully watched, for the heat must not be too strong at first or the clay would crack. Kindling was added slowly to keep the fires even, so that the pots would be tempered evenly on all sides. After a strong firing, the pot was waterproof and would not crack in the hearth. This important step was handled only by the older, more experienced women. The younger ones carefully listened to their instructions, for the time would come when one of them would have to teach this craft to the younger women.

The fires burned by the riverbanks late into the evening. A quiet singing was heard over the river—the oldest of the women was calling the spirits to keep the new pots from breaking and to cause them always to be filled with plenty of good food.

Everyone forgot about Meku. He had quietly slipped away and was pinching himself as hard as he could to teach himself to bear any kind of pain silently.

Chapter 12

Soon after the initiation of the new hunters, the men began preparations for a seal hunt in the waters of the bay. Nearly all the men cherished the unlikely hope of getting a whale also, but such good fortune came perhaps only once in ten years.

The hunters made their own fishing tackle and fishing clothes. Nothing worn or used during the fishing expedition was allowed to be touched by a woman's hand.

In the morning, a band of hunters headed toward the seashore where, in a dried-up arm of the river Vig, the fishing boats of the village were stored. It was too early in the season to go into the water, but the men had to undertake the difficult and painstaking work of fashioning a new boat. Three years ago they had selected a huge oak tree with a straight fat trunk. Using stone chisels, they had scraped off the bark in thick circles at the base of the tree. Leaves no longer covered its branches, for the summer heat and the winter frosts had taken their toll. It was time to fell the tree. The earth was cleared away from the roots and a fire was built under them. The fire slowly licked the knotty, damp roots, first charring them on all sides, then burning through to the core. Finally, with a great crack, the oak fell to the ground breaking its branches. It took many more days for the hunters to burn the tree in two, separating the smooth lower trunk from the branchy upper part. The hunters patiently trimmed the ends of the thick trunk, and then began to burn out the inner core. In a fire made nearby, they heated stones until they were red-hot and then laid them along the trunk. And then, some with stone hammers and some with adzes, they chipped away the charred layer and again heated the stones and repeated the process. The men toiled for a long time, until the huge block of wood had been turned into a clumsy boat. It was very heavy, but steady in the waves of the great sea.

The other boats needed fixing. Pine tar, mixed with fine sand, was rubbed over the cracks; deep holes were dug in the sand under the boats and small fires of tarry pine logs were burned in the holes to cover the boats with smoke. The greasy soot covering the bottom and sides protected the boat from seepage.

The hunters who remained in camp were busy also. They prepared special clothes for the sea hunt. Made from the skins of seal and walrus, they were usually warm and, more importantly, waterproof. They began work at sunup and labored until dark.

Only Kremen took no part in the activities by the sea or the work in camp. Once in a while he came to look things over, gave a few orders and then left. He was preparing the weapons needed for the hunt—harpoons and sharp points for spears and axes. According to custom, only the Glavni could make the weapons necessary for the hunt. In order for the spears to be straight and fly true they needed evenly balanced stone points. The bone harpoon needed to be straight and sharp, with notches on each side carved exactly alike. But Kremen's left hand had been maimed by a bear when he was still young, and while it had almost unnatural strength, the fingers had never been very nimble again. Now his fingers were also stiffened and bent with age, and the weapons he made were worse and worse every year. When the hunters had received new weapons from Kremen in the past, they had just muttered in distress but had not dared to speak out. But this time when the weapons were handed out, Au took his new bone harpoon from Kremen and, looking it over carefully for a long time, handed it back to Kremen saying, "How could anyone hit an animal with this harpoon? Give me another one."

"This one will do for the likes of you," said Kremen angrily. "Take it, for you will not get another one."

There was nothing to be done and Au took the crooked harpoon. But it was this particular hunt that was to decide Au's fate—for five years after his initiation it was at last the right of a hunter to throw his harpoon during the sea hunt. If he missed twice, he never got another chance and was relegated to the function of oarsman.

Au headed toward the swamp to practice throwing his harpoon at the clumps of moss. Out of five tries he hit his mark only once. Still he threw it again and again until finally, giving up in anger, he flung the weapon to the ground and sat down on a rock. That is how Liok found him sometime later. Seeing his friend, Liok understood immediately that he was troubled. Au said nothing in answer to Liok's questions and just handed the harpoon to the young shaman. Although Liok was not a hunter, even a child could distinguish a bad weapon from a good one. "Wait for me here," he said and ran off to his dugout.

One of the shamans who had inhabited the dugout before him had obviously liked to pass his time by fashioning weapons out of bone. And when he had first moved in,

Liok had found a birch box concealed in the dugout containing a knife made from the ribs of a lynx, a couple of arrowheads, and a long, straight, sharp harpoon. He had told no one of his find, secretly hoping that he would someday get a chance to use them himself. But for a friend like Au, who had warned him about Fox Paw's treachery . . . He grabbed the harpoon and ran back to where Au was waiting.

Au could not tear his eyes away from the wonderful weapon, for he had never seen the like of it. Uncertainly, as if he couldn't believe his luck, he took hold of the harpoon and threw it at the nearest clump of moss. The harpoon struck in the very center. He threw it again at a greater distance, and again the harpoon landed exactly where he had aimed it.

"You are a great friend! . . . A great friend!" repeated Au happily, but even as he said this his face clouded over in despair. He handed the harpoon back to Liok and said, "Take it back. Kremen will never let me keep it. The custom is that hunters can only take their weapons from the Glavni."

But Liok had thought of that also. He leaned over and whispered so quietly in Au's ear that not a beast, not a bird, not even a tiny mosquito could hear what he said. Slowly, the young hunter's face lit up and finally he laughed. "That is what we will do," said Liok aloud, thrusting the harpoon inside his own fur cape.

Everything was ready for going out to sea. Now it was only necessary to wait for a favorable time. The hunt at sea was the most dangerous kind. The firm ground was dependable, but not so the sea, where the boats would be raised high on the crest of a wave then tossed down between huge mountains of water. A wounded walrus or whale could easily overturn the frail boat; a sudden storm could drive the boat so far out to sea that the hunters would never return home.

Thus, from generation to generation, the people of the village had accumulated a lore of signs and omens. The old hunters could guess if the wind would be blowing in the right direction on the following day, or if a storm was hiding behind a small cloud at the edge of the sky. These signs had often saved the hunters from disaster, but there were also other signs. They must listen also to the bidding of the spirits, who spoke to them through the shaman.

The hunters were waiting for a decisive word from Liok, but the young shaman did not know what to do. He tried making magic in his dugout, to summon the spirits, but he neither saw nor heard anything. Then he remembered his proven method. He chiseled out the images of a whale and a seal on the Sacred Cliff so that the hunters would first try out their luck on these. But before deciding on a day, he sought out old Niuk on the path leading to the camp. Old Niuk had lived through many winters and had gone on many hunts, and Liok engaged him in a conversation about the weather and the sea voyage, wherein the simplehearted old man revealed to the young shaman much needed information. Then Liok headed to the hunters' camp, to speak to Kremen. "Call the hunters to the Sacred Cliff for the hunting ritual," he told the Glavni.

The hunters gathered at the rapids, curiously examining the new images on the cliff. Liok stepped forward and said in a singsong voice, "My spirits have told me to make the images of the animals you will be hunting. Tomorrow you will go out to sea." Everything proceeded according to established ritual. The animals on the cliff were very big and the hunters had no trouble hitting their mark. "It will be a big catch," the hunters thought happily. At the end of the ceremony, Liok raised his arms and proclaimed loudly, "Hunters! Yesterday the hunchbacked Roko came to visit me and brought a gift. He told me to give it to the hunter who will be throwing the harpoon for the first time this year. Tell me, Glavni, who will that be?"

Kremen frowned, sensing something not to his liking. But how could he guess the cunning of this shaman? "Au," he muttered unwillingly.

"Come here, Au!" said Liok ceremoniously. "Stand beside me and stretch out your arms to the protector and Friend of the Hunters, Roko." Au did as he was told and Liok handed the harpoon to him. "Take this gift from the spirits."

The hunters, forgetting that they were in a sacred place, milled around Au noisily like children, elbowing each other to get a better look at the gift from Roko. Kremen was crimson with rage, for he had instantly recognized the harpoon. Many years ago, in the days of his youth, he had had a friend who had become a shaman. He had made weapons out of bone, planning to give them to Kremen, but they had had a fight and the weapons remained in the shaman's dugout. Kremen had forgotten about them, and now the crafty young shaman had convinced the hunters that it was a gift from Roko.

"No one is allowed to break with the tradition," roared the voice of the old hunter. "Weapons are given by me." And with rage, he reached for the harpoon. "Throw it into the rapids!" he ordered Au.

The young hunter pressed the harpoon to his chest. A murmur passed through the crowd. How could such a wonderful weapon be thrown away!

"It is a gift from the spirits!" shouted Liok. "Do you want to bring their wrath down on all the hunters?" The hunters shook their heads in agreement. And old Niuk stepped up to the Glavni and said, "How can hunters go out to sea against the wishes of the spirits? Not even you, Glavni, are allowed to anger them."

Kremen was silent as the hunters departed. Then only Kremen and the shaman remained on the cliff. The old man asked, "Did you tell Roko the night of the initiation of the new hunters?"

"I asked him to go," answered Liok.

"Why didn't he give the harpoon then? You say it is a gift from him, don't you?" And his eyes, not looking like those of an old man, were fixed on the face of the young shaman.

"What is he guessing? What does he know?" wondered Liok. And instead of answering the old man Liok asked, "Has Roko told you that you should initiate me into the hunters? All of our shamans have been old, only I am young. My feet are fast, my hands are strong."

"No," answered Kremen, "you will never be a hunter, you will never know our secrets. When you died you would tell everything to the animals." And the old man looked at the young one so angrily that the boy became afraid.

Chapter 13

ON THE NIGHT before the hunters went out to sea, the sun had hardly set when Kremen ordered the hunters to go to sleep—a vigilant eye and a sure hand belonged only to well-rested men.

The women in the village, on the other hand, did not even lie down. Neither the usual chatter nor the cry of children was heard, although there was a great deal being done. Children brought water from the river in bags made of elk gut; the old women were busy handing out dried fish and smoked duck breasts from the storehouse to the other women. Each had to store up as much food and water as possible, for while the hunters remained at sea, the women and children had to stay quietly in their dugouts. If they did this, they believed that the sea animals too would be still. With the first rays of the sun, the women, having finished their preparations, crawled into their sleeping bags with their children.

Only quiet whispers could be heard as the mothers warned the children for the last time of all the things they were forbidden to do. The village looked as though deserted.

The hunters gathered in their camp. They took all their clothing, and then, as if hiding from an enemy, they one by one slipped out of the gate. Shivering in the morning cold, they walked completely naked through the forest, not daring even to wave away the mosquitoes.

At a sign from Kremen, Bei separated himself from the file of hunters and quickly ran to the shaman's dugout. From a distance he threw some pebbles at the covering and Liok came out immediately. Seeing that his brother wore no clothes, Liok immediately started undressing. But Bei waved his arms at him—a shaman was not supposed to wear special clothing for the sea hunt. Liok nodded his head to show that he understood. It was forbidden to speak—the birds and the animals, the insects and fish would discover the hunters' plans from the people's speech. As long as not a word was spoken, there was no need to fear that the sea animals would know of the attack.

Bei took his brother to the clearing where the other hunters awaited them, and they continued on their way together. It was good to walk through the pines on a quiet morning. The forest smelled of conifers, ledum, and many blooming flowers and grasses. The sun, now higher in the sky, was filling the forest with such hot rays that the pine tar melted and ran down the trunks in hidden streams.

Liok saw for the first time on the bodies of the experienced hunters the whitish scars from teeth or claws and the dark marks left by blows from elk horn. Kremen especially had many scars.

Liok wanted to ask many things of Bei or Au, but until the hunters had donned their fishing clothes, not a word must be spoken. Silently, they stole through the bushes and the trees, trying not to crack a single twig underfoot.

When they reached an opening in the cliffs by the bay, Kremen signaled that Liok should wait for them outside and then disappeared into the narrow divide. One by one, the other hunters slipped through the opening and Liok was alone. He sat at first under a tree and then, unable to stifle his curiosity, quietly crawled up to the crack in the granite wall. Carefully moving aside the bushes that concealed the crevice, he saw a small clearing surrounded by large old fir trees. Birchwood boxes hung from their shaggy branches, and beneath one of the fir trees, which stood apart from all the rest, Liok could see Kremen's enormous body. The tree that towered over him was distinguished from the others by the trunk, which split off at the top into separate parts. His eyes firmly shut, the old man was putting on his clothes for the fishing expedition, while the other hunters dressed themselves beneath the other trees. Their eyes too were closed and their lips were moving—for they were whispering incantations. Those who had already dressed themselves were painting their faces with paints from large clay pots.

Liok watched enviously as his contemporaries performed these hunting rituals side by side with the experienced hunters. Had he not become a shaman, he would be right there with them, instead of sneaking up and spying on them. Liok crawled back and sadly sat and waited under a tree.

Soon, one after another, the hunters returned, dressed in waterproof clothing. Their faces were painted beyond recognition, for after the hunt the spirits of the dead sea animals would hunt for those who had killed them, but the hunters would by then have washed the paint off their faces and the spirits would not be able to recognize them.

They went on their way. Now it was permissible to whisper quietly and Liok heard many unfamiliar words. Pulling Bei by his sleeve he led him aside and began asking questions. Bei explained that "mountain of fat and meat" meant whale, that "old man with a moustache" was a walrus, "motley mouse" was a seal, and "white worm" was a white whale. "We cannot call them by their real names," explained the young hunter, "for if they heard these then they would know that we are coming to hunt them and would swim far out to sea, or go far down into the deeps where no harpoon could reach them."

Soon they came out on the boulder-strewn channel of the Vig River. Between the trunks of the pine trees they could see the sparkling ripples of the nearby water. The heavy boats were ready. The hunters dragged them to the water by placing heavy rollers made of round slim logs beneath them. The young hunters quickly brought out from secret hiding places masts, oars, and sails made of animal skins sewn together. The lively spirit of the hunters was infectious, and Liok wanted to help them drag the boats to the water and set up the masts. He had already taken hold of a side of the nearest boat when Kremen shouted, "Do not forget that you are a shaman, not a hunter." Liok sadly stepped aside.

When the boats were finally afloat in the shallow water, the hunters began to seat themselves. Liok headed over to the boat where Au was sitting, but again the harsh voice of the Glavni brought him to a halt. "The shaman comes with me!" And Liok had to sit in the same boat with Kremen.

Whispering some incantations to bring them luck, Kremen tied a cross pole, with the sail attached, to the mast. As the sail filled, the boat shuddered as if alive, and sped out to sea. A fair wind was blowing and the four oarsmen, sitting on the bottom of the boat, had nothing to do. One of them was holding the cross pole with the sail and turning it first to one side, then to another, steering the boat in the direction that Kremen indicated. The old man sat in the front pressing his chest up against the prow. With his hand above his eyes, he looked vigilantly into the distance. Beside him, covered with a piece of deerskin, lay his harpoon with a crooked but carefully sharpened point. A long, thin leather rope lay coiled in a ring and tied to it was a sealskin balloon filled with air.

The boats traveled in a large semicircle. In the center was Kremen's boat and beside it, staying slightly behind, was the boat with Au at the prow.

Liok had never been out to the open sea and was thrilled that he had gotten to go on the hunt with the hunters. He sat near Kremen with his back against the mast and marvelled at the beauty of the strip of wooded land to the left and at the quiet beauty of the open sea.

Large sea gulls passed overhead from time to time. The people gazed at them with worried expressions: the sea gull, that unwelcome spy, could see everything and tell the animals. For this very reason the hunters had carefully hidden their fishing gear.

A small cloud traveled across the path of the sun's rays and the blinding ripples darkened a little. Suddenly Kremen strained his whole body and quickly shoved his hand under the deerskin. Liok looked in the direction that Kremen was staring and saw a sparkling white object not very far away from them. It turned over in the water and disappeared with a great splash.

"The white worm," whispered Kremen. Soon the white spot sparkled again. The animal was approaching them. "Your spirits bring us luck," said one of the oarsmen to Liok. "How quickly the game comes to us." Kremen's face, distorted with rage, turned on the speaking man. The Glavni silently shook his fist at the man, for premature boasting could chase away the entire catch.

The hunt began. The hunters had to get within throwing range of the whale, without scaring it off. The animal gamboled in the water unheedful of the approaching boat. Bending its body into a bow, it tumbled and somersaulted among the small waves.

Hiding behind the sides, the oarsmen carefully rowed closer to the animal. Several times the animal's white side appeared quite close to the boat, but then diving down, it would appear again far in the distance. Again, the oarsmen patiently rowed closer to the playful animal. Finally its glossy long body appeared almost next to the boat, and piercing the air with a whistle Kremen's harpoon lodged in the animal's side.

The white whale whirled madly, trying to dislodge the sharp weapon. Now came the tensest, most dangerous moment of the hunt. The wounded beast could easily break the boat in two like a piece of straw. Fortunately it dived and surfaced a small distance away. The hunters never took their eyes off the flailing animal for a moment. "Will it land on the shore or go out to sea?" was the question in all their minds.

"To sea!" exclaimed Kremen with a groan, "to sea." Diving down for a final time, the white whale made a headlong dash for the sea. The glistening sides of the animal, now pink from blood, appeared farther and farther away.

The hunt had begun with bad luck. And everyone now recalled the untimely words spoken by the oarsman—bragging about the catch even as it had slipped away. Kremen, out of control, stood up. Stepping across Liok he swung his arm and struck the offending oarsman on his head with such force that blood spouted from his nose. Could there have happened a disaster worse than this?

Recovering himself instantly, Kremen stooped over and lowered himself into his place. The oarsman held his nose in his hands, but the blood spilled over his chin and chest. The hunters in the neighboring boats watched with horror. Not waiting for directions from Kremen, the oarsmen turned the boat around and headed back to shore. The other boats followed. Kremen just sat there, his head lowered, his face covered with his hands, for his action had caused the sun to see the blood of a kinsman. Kremen was pitiful to look at now. Knowing that there was no excuse for his action, the Glavni had lost all authority. Everyone avoided him and the oarsman—for until they had performed a rite of purification they were both considered unclean. No one must touch them.

Old Niuk, who was now in charge, ordered Liok to go off into the forest for the night and to return early in the morning. The hunters' rites were not to be witnessed by the uninitiated. Liok was disappointed. All day he had felt himself a hunter like the rest, had waited with the same impatience to see if the animal would appear, had grieved just as strongly when the white whale had gone out to sea. He went reluctantly into the forest. He spent the night under the rotting hull of a boat that was no longer seaworthy.

When Liok returned in the morning, the purification rite had long been finished. Only thin streams of smoke remained from five fires arranged in a circle.

The hunters were readying themselves to go out to sea again. Kremen, gloomy and preoccupied, was back in charge. There was no wind, the sails hung limply from the cross bows, and the boats had to be rowed. First one set of oarsmen rowed, then they were relieved by a second set. Kremen sat again in the prow, vigilantly looking out into the distance. The gloomy morning turned into a gloomy afternoon. Kremen sat motionlessly in his place, staring hopefully into the distance. But no matter how much the boat furrowed the still water, no animal showed itself to them. Once in the distance they caught sight of a whale, but it was too far away and soon disappeared from sight. In the evening, the men returned to shore, exhausted and discouraged.

They made fires, ate their smoked duck meat, and immediately fell asleep.

The third day at sea was no better than the first two. Au never even needed to reach for his harpoon. The hunters shot sidelong glances in Kremen's direction. It was apparent that the purification rite had not helped. The crime of spilling a kinsman's blood was a grave one.

At a council of hunters it was decided that they should return to camp and after a day resume the hunt. They dragged the heavy boats inland, as if the hunt were finished. Let the animals think that the hunters were leaving and were not going to return. In the clearing between the cliffs they removed their hunting clothes and washed the ocher off their faces. Then they gloomily returned to camp.

Barely had they turned in for the night, when beyond the gate they heard a piercing shout of an old woman calling Kremen's name. Kremen went out and found the new High Koldunya. "I can see that you have had no luck on the sea," she said to him. Kremen became furious—was he not to have any peace even here! He waved his hand angrily at her and turned to go.

"Wait, Glavni," whispered the Koldunya, "if you really have not caught anything, I will tell you whose fault it is. An event in the village has angered the spirits." And she told him how two days ago, a little boy, son of Spark in whose dugout Au lived, ran out of his dugout. Not heeding his mother's frightened calls (she did not dare go after him), he ran around all morning, amusing himself with the fact that no one could catch him.

Ordering the High Koldunya to call together the women and children at the Sacred Cliff, Kremen returned to camp. "We must all go to the rapids," he ordered, barely concealing the satisfaction he was feeling, "you will discover who is guilty of chasing the animals out of the bay."

Soon everyone was gathered on the two small islands by the cliff. In the clear twilight of the northern summer night the faces of the men and women appeared chalk white, and the water of the rapids, pitch black. It was very quiet, for no one dared speak a word. A heavy feeling of impending doom hovered over the people.

Kremen called Tibu over with a sign and whispered something in his ear. The boy crossed over to the island where the women were and returned leading little Kao by the hand. Liok, standing on the cliff, noticed how Au twitched with anxiety, when Tibu led the little boy up to Kremen. Au started toward the cliff, as if to seek the help of his friend the shaman, and then changing his mind ran up to old Niuk. Au whispered something in his ear, but the old man just shook his head.

Spark's sobbing was heard from the island of women. Kremen lifted the little boy high into the air. Kao smiled happily to be in the arms of the Glavni himself. But the old man spoke harshly, "He has brought misfortune to the village and he will be punished." Kremen walked over to the edge of the cliff carrying the now-frightened child in his outstretched arms. Everyone froze. Even Spark's sobbing came to a halt. Over the din of the rapids, the Glavni called out, "Spirit of the Rapids, take this disobedient one to yourself and send us luck in our hunt."

And so the old man had dealt with the guilty offender. The hunters silently trailed back to their camp. Last of all came Au, staggering with grief. The women returned quietly to the village clutching their frightened children to their breasts. The young mother had to be dragged away forcibly.

Chapter 14

ONCE MORE the hunters gathered silently at the old river-bed. They dragged the heavy boats down to the sea once more and took the mast, oars, and sails from their hiding places again. To anyone watching them it would have looked as if the hunters were going out to sea for the first time this year. And which sea animal could have guessed that these were the same hunters who were out a few days before, for their faces were now painted in a completely different way.

A fresh wind blew from the southwest. The hunters raised the sails on the boats and, speeding out into the bay, they sailed north, parallel to the coastline. The boats again formed a large semicircle, with Kremen's boat in the center followed closely by the boat containing Au. And although Kremen appeared imperturbable as usual, Liok knew that he was deeply worried.

The time for the sea hunt was very short. If they did not store up enough meat and fat from these animals now, the village would be starving long before the return of another spring. Kremen also worried that his reputation as a hunter who never failed would be diminished among his people. The bad luck of the first few days was no longer his fault, but in order to regain their previous confidence in him, he himself had to bring in a large catch.

At midday the wind died down and the oarsmen reluctantly picked up their heavy oars. The boats moved slowly across the quiet waves. The rowing shift had changed for the fourth time, when in the distance, three white whales appeared. Kremen pressed his whole body against the nose of the boat, as if to help make it go faster, while the oarsmen redoubled their efforts.

Kremen's boat, leaving the others behind, began to approach the group of playing animals. But a second boat came up even with his. Au was at the head of its prow. Tensing all his muscles, he raised his new harpoon. The white whales continued to play among the waves.

As the two boats raced side by side, Au's boat began to take the lead. Kremen gnashed his teeth in anger. People had been talking about the sureness of the young man's eye and the quickness of his hand, and now he carried a wonderful weapon. If he, Kremen, missed because of the crooked point of his harpoon and the young man hit the animal, then disgrace would finally fall on his old head.

Now Au's boat completely blocked the path of the old hunter's boat. Leaning his right knee against the side of the boat and bending forward slightly, Au drew back the arm holding the harpoon, ready to send it shooting into the animal's fat white body.

Not saying a word, Kremen hurriedly made a sign to his oarsmen. They obediently turned the boat sharply, its nose pointing right at the center of Au's boat. Au's own oarsmen pulled frantically to move it out of the way, but it was too late and the boats collided. Au staggered from the unexpected impact and at that very moment Kremen threw his harpoon. But the strong impact of one boat against the other took away the sureness of his hand and his harpoon merely grazed the animal's back and did not lodge in it. The white whale dived beneath the surface of the water, and its playmates, sensing danger, also disappeared.

The boats continued to ply the waves, but in vain, for the water remained empty of game. A wind sprung up just before evening. One strong gust followed another, tearing the foam from the rising waves and spraying the boats and the hunters. It was the beginning of a storm, and though the winds blew them into shore rather than out to sea, their boats were battered against the rocks.

When the wet and exhausted hunters had sat down around a fire, old Niuk said, "The spirits are angry at us."

"Yes, we have angered them," replied an oarsman from Kremen's boat and threw the Glavni a sidelong glance. The other hunters all looked steadily at the old hunter, waiting to see what he would say. But Kremen was silent. What could a man say who twice had gone against the better interests of his people?

The storm did not abate. A foul night fell, and the younger hunters began to turn in for the night. Two of them cleverly lay down on the ground first, heads touching. The others lay across the first two, and the rest followed suit. Liok looked enviously at the hunters. According to custom, the shaman must sleep away from other men. He walked a distance, dug out a space between the roots of an old fir tree, dragged some moss into this burrow, and settled in for the night.

The old men remained around the fire, throwing in kindling and averting their heads from the billows of acrid smoke that came their way when a gust of wind sprang up. For a long time they discussed something in half whispers and fell asleep only toward morning.

By morning the wind had died down and the waves were quieter. The hunters awoke and put out the fires carefully, for they were forbidden to leave even one spark going in the fire. What if a stranger appeared and forced the fire of their people to serve him?

When Liok crawled out of his burrow and approached the hunters, Kremen called, "I have need of your advice, shaman! Do your spirits agree that we should mollify the water by giving it some sweet meat? I think without this we will have no luck."

Liok did not understand what Kremen was getting at. "Sweet meat?" What could that be? Perhaps he was right? If they gave the sea some sweet meat then they would have better luck. Liok almost opened his mouth in agreement, when he saw the worried expressions on the faces of his brother and Au, and understood that he was in some kind of danger.

"So what do your spirits say?" asked the old man impatiently. "Why not give some sweet meat to the sea?"

"Wait! My spirits have not spoken to me yet," answered Liok. Then he recalled an old tale by his mother about a terrible spirit who swallowed people alive and called them "sweet meat." So that was what the old man had in mind!

"No!" answered Liok slowly but clearly, "my spirits do not want to give sweet meat to the sea. My spirits have told me something else. They have said, 'We are angry with Kremen! He loves himself more than he loves his people. Let him go away. Let Au be the Glavni for this hunt. We will send big game to Au.' "

"You dare to banish me!" roared Kremen, stepping toward the youth. But Bei stepped in front of Liok, shielding him with his body. "How can you disobey the will of the spirits?" he shouted at the Glavni. "Doesn't the outcome of the hunt depend on them?"

"Have you, Glavni, forgotten the ancient tradition?" spoke up old Niuk. "He who has proven himself guilty before his people must step aside until the spirits are no longer angry. Go to the camp and wait there until the end of the hunt. Do you agree, hunters?"

A resounding "Yes!" came from the hunters.

Kremen drooped his head. Their unanimity was a sentence. The Glavni went over to the weapons and picked up his harpoon. The departing Chief Hunter had to hand his weapon to the one who was taking his place. But Kremen could not control himself; he did not hand his weapon to Au, but threw it to the ground with such force that not only did the tip break off, but the entire harpoon broke into splinters. Then, not looking at anyone he walked slowly and deliberately into the forest. The old man had lived for a very long time and never once in his life could he remember when the Glavni had been banished from the hunt. . . .

The hunters again began preparations to go out to sea. While the oarsmen dragged the heavy boats out to the shore, Liok noticed that Au wore a solemn expression on his face, and the shaman asked quietly, "Are you not pleased that you are now the Glavni at this hunt?"

"Kremen will never forget this and he will bring ruin upon me."

"Tell me, Au," asked Liok, "did he want to kill me today?"

"Your spirits have saved you again," Au answered him in a barely audible whisper. "That is how the old shaman died. He struggled in the waves for a long time, our boats had left him far behind, but we could still hear his cries. But that day the spirits sent us two seals, and the old men said that the sweet meat had enticed them. I think we would have caught the seals anyway."

Liok followed Au into his boat. The storm had driven small fish into the bay, and these were the favorite food of whales. No sooner had the hunters gotten out to the open sea, when they saw four silvery fountains in the distance. Whales! The hunters did not dare to even dream of such luck. Their clumsy, heavy boats could not catch up with the swift whale even in the strongest breeze. But luck smiled on them this time, and the whales swam in their direction. Each hunter was praying to the spirits to send them close and at the same time each hunter feared just that, for one flick of the enormous tail could smash their boat, and a wave raised by the enormous animal could turn it over. Liok watched as an enormous whale approached them, then lifted its tail into the air and, raising a column of foam and water, disappeared beneath the surface.

"Gone!" Liok almost cried out in despair. "Gone, gone," thought all the hunters. "All that meat and fat, gone."

But they were mistaken. The water churned once more nearby and suddenly a blue back appeared. Au threw his harpoon that very instant, and the weapon lodged firmly in the animal's back.

The long leather rope that was tied to the harpoon was thrown into the water along with the blown up sealskin balloon. Luck was still with the hunters. The wounded whale raced right by their boats, beating the water with his tail and raising huge waves. Far to the side of the racing animal the blown-up sealskin balloon danced among the waves.

Where would it go? If it went to sea, then they would lose all that food. If it went toward the shore, then the people of the village would be well fed for the winter. At first the whale traveled in large circles, and the hunters held their breath each time the whale turned toward the sea. But suddenly the whale gave one last splash with its tail and sped straight into the shallow waters of the shoreline. All the boats turned and followed, and the hunters waved their oars in the air, shouting at the top of their lungs.

Before long they were climbing up the huge hulk of flesh on their hands and knees, dancing on the expanse of whale back, sliding on the slippery black skin, and falling into the water only to climb back up again. A long time went by before the hunters calmed down. Some were dripping wet, some were covered with scratches and bruises, and others were hoarse from shouting. Such good luck did not come often. The people in the village would long remember this event. This year would be referred to as "The year Au killed the whale."

The people of the village called themselves "The Children of the Whale," and as a sign of this always wore a bit of whale skin in their clothes. They did not dare touch the delicious meat and fat until they had gotten the forgiveness of the whale's spirit.

The sun had barely set behind the forest when the hunters hurriedly made an enormous bonfire. Then laying themselves down on the ground and pretending to be asleep, they started to snore loudly. Something dark crawled toward the enormous hulk of the dead whale. This was young Ziu, imitating a whale. Suddenly, Bei, painted beyond recognition, appeared brandishing a harpoon. Dancing all around him, Bei started to attack the "whale" who was swimming across the sand. The sharp point of his spear scratched the "whale's" arm and drops of blood fell on the ground. The "whale" shouted loudly. Then the "sleeping" hunters awoke and fell on the painted hunter, beating him with their fists.

Thus the hunters professed to the spirit of the whale their innocence of the whale's death and their anger with its killer. Indeed, they professed their anger so zealously that Bei lost no time in falling to the ground and playing dead.

Having made peace with the spirit of the whale, the

hunters busied themselves around the mountain of fat and meat.

For an entire week the hunters stored away the meat and fat of the whale in wide deep holes, which were reinforced with wooden poles so they would not cave in. When a hole was filled with alternating layers of meat and fat, it was covered with a layer of birch bark, then flat stones, and finally it was covered with earth. In this way the meat would sour, but it would not rot. Though smelly and bitter, it would not turn poisonous. In the winter, during the time of famine, the people would gratefully eat these strong-smelling, fat pieces of meat.

Even the whale's enormous ribs were put to good use in the village—better supports for dugouts than whale ribs could not be found anywhere. The ribs were semicircular and even; their thin, curved ends would be fastened together, while the blunt end would be buried in the ground. They never rotted like wooden poles, which needed to be replaced often. They made a sturdy dwelling that could survive for several generations.

The hunters were pleased. Ten holes, each the depth and width of a man's height, were filled to the top with food. It would not be necessary to go out to sea again this year. They had all eaten as much as they could eat. Now they wanted to return as quickly as possible to the village, to let the women know the happy news, and to return to their own camp where they could sleep sheltered from the wind and the rain and from the hordes of mosquitoes.

Near the holes, the hunters erected a column of flat stones to identify the spot in the winter snow. Then they got back into their boats and headed south for home, keeping close to the shore all the journey. The next day, the familiar cliff came into sight and the hunters entered the bay by the village.

Chapter 15

THE HUNTERS APPROACHED the field in front of the village joyously and with triumphant shouts. Hearing their voices, the women and children came out of the dugouts. They surrounded the hunters in a tight circle, and the old women nodded their heads approvingly as they listened to old Niuk tell about the ten deep holes filled with meat. The younger women and the adolescents showered the hunters with questions. Tibu, filled with pride, lay on the ground to show the exclaiming women how the whale had beat his enormous tail threatening to sink the boat he had been in. The older girls did not take their eyes off Au, who had become a great hero. Au himself looked around proudly, searching the crowd until his eyes met those of Spark, and he smiled gently at her. In her happiness for him, she temporarily forgot her grief.

Only Kremen was missing from the field. He could hear the joyous shouting from the village, but the old man, once the greatest hunter of his people, was ashamed to listen with the women to the praises of other hunters. He sat in his dugout in the hunters' camp awaiting the return of the men.

Many many years had passed since Kremen had first

become the Glavni. Instant obedience had been his, and praise for the success of every hunt had been his as well. Now it was a bitter thing for the proud old man to hear of the luck that had befallen the young hunter Au.

While Au was telling him about the hunt, Kremen was thinking about how to make the hunters believe in his power again and how to destroy this usurper. Having listened to the end of the story, he commanded the young hunter, "Bring me your harpoon. You have done your work. You don't need it anymore."

At first hearing, there seemed nothing unusual about Kremen's order. It had always been so—if anyone temporarily took the place of the Glavni during a hunt, he received the weapons of the Glavni and was bound to return them at the end of the hunt. But Kremen had broken his own harpoon. Au was confused. Finally he remembered the crooked harpoon that the Glavni had given him before they went out to sea. He brought that to Kremen.

"Not this one," said Kremen, barely glancing at it. "Bring me the harpoon that struck the whale."

Au turned white. "That harpoon was given me by the spirits," he whispered in a halting voice. "How can I give it away?"

"I am still the Glavni!" Kremen reminded him. "You dare not disobey me."

"Perhaps you will break it the way you broke your own," Au answered firmly. "Who knows what thoughts you have in your head."

"That is not your affair. You must obey," repeated the old man menacingly.

"No!" answered Au, decisively. "What hunter would give such a weapon up for ruin?"

Many eyes regarded Kremen disapprovingly. Au's answer expressed the feelings of all the hunters—what hunter, indeed, would give up such a superlative weapon to ruin?

There was a long silence. But Au did not back down, and finally the old man spoke, "Custom rules that all hunters must obey the Glavni. You have sat for one day in my place and now you think you need no longer obey me. But there cannot be two Glavnis in the village. Tomorrow, at the rapids, our dead ancestors will decide which of us alone will be Glavni."

No one had ever broken Kremen's strong grip, but Au had no choice. If he refused to appear tomorrow at the rapids, he would be branded a coward and forever banished from the village. But even if such a shameful punishment did not await him, he would still accept Kremen's challenge.

"Let it be as you say," Au answered hoarsely, looking the old man straight in the eyes.

No sooner had Au spoken these words, than Bei, sitting near the entrance of the dugout, silently lifted the curtain and slipped out.

Liok was once more sitting in the lonely dwelling of the shaman. The anxious, joyous days when he had been almost a hunter were over. And now it was even more difficult for him to resume his solitary existence. A fire at least would provide some companionship, and Liok impatiently rubbed a stick against a fire board. But the wood was damp and crumbled beneath his fingers, and it took a long time before a wisp of smoke appeared beneath the sharp end of his fire drill. Suddenly he heard his brother call outside the dugout. "Wait," Liok called, "I'm just making a fire."

"The fire can wait. Come out quickly!"

His brother's voice was so worried that Liok ran out to him immediately. "A terrible thing has happened. What will we do . . . ?" Bei began in a halting voice, and told

Liok about the events at the camp. Liok became as frightened as his brother.

"What can be done? The old man will kill Au."

"But Au cannot refuse!" shouted Bei in despair and grabbed Liok by the arm. "Listen, brother, the harpoon was a gift from Roko. Apparently the Friend of the Hunters does not know what Kremen has in mind. Tell him about it, and perhaps he will come to Au's defense."

Liok shook his head pensively. "I don't know if Roko can . . . But you have done well to tell me right away. And now go back before your absence is noticed. I will think on it."

"You are cunning, you will think of something," exclaimed Bei and headed toward camp.

Liok sat for a long time on the stone in front of his dugout, before an idea came to him. His plan required, first of all, a large quantity of fresh blood. Where could he get it? Should he go into the forest to search for a deer? Too long and too risky. What if he didn't get one? At last he leaped up from the stone and ran off into the forest. Running almost all the way, he reached a small shallow lake hidden by a thick growth of prickly bushes. Children were forbidden to swim in this water, but Liok had tried it a long time ago, and he had then sworn that he would never go near it again. Just the memory of it was enough to send cold shivers down his spine.

But now he decisively waded into the murky water. Something cold touched one leg, then something tickled his other leg. Liok screwed up his face but stayed in the water.

Only when he felt that the skin on his legs was pierced in many places did he carefully wade back to shore. He was covered with black leeches from the bottom of his foot to the top of his knees. Liok ripped some bark off a nearby birch and fashioned a kind of basket from it. Then he sat and patiently waited for the cold slippery creatures to suck themselves full of his blood and fall off. As they swelled, their color turned from black to deep red, and one by one they fell off his legs into the basket. The young shaman became slightly dizzy; he wanted to lie down but there was no time. Night was already falling in the forest. Quickly, Liok headed toward the now familiar place between the cliffs where the hunters stored their hunting clothes. Slipping between the sheer faces of the cliffs he entered the secret clearing and instantly found the prominent spruce with its separated top branches, Kremen's tree.

At dawn, in one of the dugouts at the edge of the village, a child awoke hearing strange and disturbing noises. He looked outside and rushing back inside began to wake his mother. The woman ran out and saw the shaman sitting nearby shaking back and forth, waving his arms in the air and in a singsong voice calling his people to gather together. The woman ran to her neighbor, the children ran to other dugouts, and soon the entire village gathered around the shaman. No one dared look directly at him. They all understood that he was talking with the spirits, and no one would dare to come between him and those with whom he visited. Liok muttered for a long time and finally, turning to the women with his eyes closed, he said, "Quickly gather the hunters together. Trouble is very near."

The frightened women sent one of the boys after the hunters. When they had all gathered together, the shaman, still keeping his eyes closed, began to speak. "I see much game in the forest, many birds on the cliffs, many fish in the sea. The spirits promise much food for the people, but terrible trouble is very near." Liok again started to mumble, then leaped up suddenly, opened his eyes very wide as if he had seen something terrible, and started waving his arms as if to keep something away.

"Bloody Khoro, why have you come to us?"

The people recoiled from the shaman—there was nothing more frightening in the world than Bloody Khoro! When he appeared, entire populations died out. The skin became covered with black spots, and people died like flies in the fall. Of all the spirits, only Khoro appeared to the people in a human guise and in human clothing.

"I see him, I see him, the terrible Khoro!" the shaman began again. "He wants to eat up all the men, all the women, and all the children! But the Friend of the Hunters is stronger than he. Help us, Roko! Tell us what to do."

Liok was silent once more. Then he raised his arms above his head, in the way of all shamans when they are delivering a message from the spirits.

"Roko has just said, 'Let the hunters go put on their hunting attire, and I will show them Bloody Khoro.' "

The hunters went directly to the place where they kept their hunting clothes. Kremen, even more morose than usual, led the way. Right now the shaman's power was greater than his. When they reached the sanctuary, Liok remained alone outside.

The time passed excruciatingly slowly for Liok. The laws of his people were sacred, and no one dared break them. Only hunters were allowed to enter the sanctuary of the hunting clothes—to disobey meant death. But what cruel death sentence must await him who has aspired to deceive the people? And that is what Liok had done.

At first no sounds came from inside the sanctuary, then someone cried out and at last the cry was taken up by many. Soon several hunters ran past Liok, taking no notice of him. The hands of many were bloodied. Only Kremen was not among the fleeing hunters. Liok knew Au was saved.

Soon the entire village knew what had happened at the hunters' sanctuary. The hunters had as usual kept their eyes closed while they changed into their hunting gear, whispering incantations. Nimble Tibu was dressed before anyone else, and on opening his eyes he saw the bloody figure of Khoro standing under the divided spruce. Khoro looked exactly like Kremen, but his clothes were covered with bloody spots. Tibu screamed . . .

Now the hunters vied with each other in telling the women what happened next, how they dealt with Bloody Khoro and how they saved the village from ruin.

One thing remained a mystery to everyone. What happened to old Kremen? The crowd turned to their shaman for the answer.

"My spirits told me that Bloody Khoro abducted Kremen and took his shape. Then he came to live among us."

Everyone accepted this explanation. Certainly, it seemed the blood that was spilled on the hunting expedition was done by Khoro, in an attempt to anger the spirits of the sea and bring hunger on the village. One of the women said that no man would ever have thrown a child into the rapids and that too must have been the work of Bloody Khoro. The old women declared that Khoro had taken over Kremen's body a long time ago, and that, they thought, was an end to it.

Chapter 16

FOR THE PEOPLE of the village the night was filled with uneasiness. The hunters had killed old Kremen, in whose body Bloody Khoro had taken refuge, but who can kill an evil spirit? Even now, Khoro must be wandering somewhere around the village. The koldunyii burned fires of juniper bushes from sunset to sunrise to ward off the terrible spirit. Tongues of flame surrounded the dugouts. Pressed close to the ground by the night damp, the smoke formed a shroud over the scene, carrying through the forest the sweetish smell of burning juniper to chase away evil spirits.

The koldunyii, their faces all painted, resembled spirits themselves. They walked tirelessly from fire to fire, beating a bone against a drum made of an animal skin stretched around a wooden hoop.

The hollow beating of their drums made the people even more frightened, and no one dared fall asleep on this night, for the soul of a person is more vulnerable in sleep than while awake. The mothers shook their children to keep them from sleeping, and the children rubbed their drooping eyes and cried loudly.

The hunting songs were heard from the hunters' camp.

The drums, the cries of children, the incantations of the koldunyii, the low bass voices of the hunters—all these merged and blended in the smoke-filled night.

Kremen had been in power for such a long time and had dealt so cruelly with dissidents, that there was no obvious candidate to take his place. Many were afraid that the vengeance of Bloody Khoro might first fall on Kremen's successor.

But the village needed a leader, and the hunters decided to let the spirits of the shaman decide who was to be the new Glavni. By sunrise, Liok was to deliver the decision of the spirits.

Such a serious undertaking required that he put on the ritual shaman attire. In order to put on the special fur vest, Liok had first to remove from around his neck the seven hanging wooden amulets—six depicting various animals, and one depicting a man. Doing this he noticed that he was missing the most important amulet, the figure of the man. Liok turned his dugout upside down looking for it, but to no avail. Though normally forbidden to remove them, Liok had found the clanking figurines bothersome, so when no one was around, he often flung them carelessly behind his back. Now such carelessness seemed to be asking its price.

A bright glow in the eastern sky spread throughout the forest, a harbinger of sunrise. Liok poured some water in a clay jar and, bending over it, began to paint his face. Having made pastes of the red ocher, green clay, and ashes with grease, he made red circles around his mouth and eyes. He painted green and black stripes on his cheeks. With each stroke his face became more frightening, and when he deliberately screwed up his mouth and eyes, what he saw reflected in the smooth water was such a monster that he himself was dumbfounded. He drew two additional stripes across his forehead, painted his arms and hands and then left his dugout in the full shaman's regalia. The flaming ball of the sun was already visible over the forest.

Seeing the young shaman in the distance the koldunyii began beating their drums louder and faster. "He's coming, he's coming," they chanted in their creaky voices.

The women and children gathered along the path where the shaman had to pass on his way to the hunters' camp. All were impatient to discover who would be the new Glavni. Liok walked along the path, his head bent and his hands covering his face. As he came nearer, the koldunyii began a new chant, "Who will it be? Who will it be? Who will it be?"

Suddenly on a boyish whim he decided to give the curious women a little scare. He removed his hands from his face and, with a terrible grimace, moved toward them.

Shrieking, the women and children scattered in all directions. The koldunyii recoiled, muttering incantations and shaking their drumsticks at him. Very pleased with himself, Liok continued on his way.

He stopped outside the tall gate of the hunters' camp to think once more of the wisdom of his decision. "Yes, that will be best," he said to himself and entered the camp for the first time.

The camp consisted of three large dugouts. The one standing in the center was called The Dwelling of the Bearded Old Man, and it was occupied by the oldest hunters, those tested on the difficult hunt for the walrus. Another one was set aside for the very youngest hunters, those just initiated. It was called Shining Arrow, which meant salmon in the hunters' language. The third dugout was for the older, more experienced hunters, who were unafraid to enter into single-handed combat with a bear. Their dugout was called The Dwelling of the Forest Man.

The hunters stood in the doorways of their dugouts, waiting to see whom the shaman's spirits had chosen.

Liok walked past the dugout of the Shining Arrow, not even glancing at the beardless youths, who only recently had been helping the women knead clay to make pots.

The old hunters nodded their heads approvingly. But Liok walked past their dugout as well, pausing only for a moment, as if in thought. The old men frowned—how could anyone from another dugout become the Glavni? But the shaman approached the dugout of the Forest Man. He signaled for the first hunter to step aside, then the second, the third, and only when he came to Au did he say, "This is the man my spirits have chosen as the Glavni."

Chapter 17

THE DAYS WERE becoming shorter and the nights were becoming longer. In the evenings large stars would appear in the darkening skies. Berries ripened. Fledglings learning to fly soared higher with each day. The gadflies were disappearing, and the deer roamed through the forest, eating mushrooms. There were such a multitude of mushrooms that deer, emaciated over the summer, quickly grew fat.

Everyone, from people to ants, was busy storing up food for the long winter. In the village there was work for everyone. Even old women wandered through the forest, through the swamps, gathering the herbs and roots known only to them, herbs and roots that could cure as well as bewitch people. The children helped the grownups—diligently searching out the sharp-smelling wild onions, digging them out and carrying them back to the village. In the days of the famine, when the people's legs swelled up and their gums began to bleed, onions had been the best medicine.

The young people were busy at the happiest task. Young men, not yet among the hunters, and young women, who had not yet moved into their own dugouts, went out together into the forest. Toward the middle of the summer, the swamps dried up somewhat, and jumping from rock to rock the young people could reach the thick growth of sedge in the center. Hidden there were flocks of molting geese.

Tibu and Liok had been considered the best catchers of molting geese. But Tibu was now a hunter and hunters do not concern themselves with such pastimes. They must knead strips of leather until they are soft and supple and they must ready hunting equipment for the winter. But Tibu so loved to hunt geese that he sought out Au to ask his permission to go for a last time after the "molters."

Au considered it. On the one hand, it was against the custom of the people; on the other hand, it would be a help if Tibu took charge of the young people on the goose hunt. And there were enough older hunters to knead the tough leather. Au agreed, and the overjoyed boy ran to catch up with his friends.

Now, it was old Niuk's habit to walk around the camp every evening to see that all was in order. Looking into the dugout of the Shining Arrow, he noticed that Tibu was not in his usual place. He immediately reported this to the Glavni, and Au explained that he had given Tibu permission to go after the molting geese.

"Why do you go against the customs of the people?" asked the old man angrily. "Is it not the place of the Glavni to enforce the observance of custom?"

Old Niuk was supported not only by the old hunters but by the younger ones as well. Who of them was not tired of kneading the wet, hard leather day after day until their hands were sore and blistered? How much more fun it would be to go hunting geese in the wild growth of lakeside sedge.

In Au's place, Kremen could have silenced them with one glance from under his knitted brows. But things were difficult for Au. The old hunters never missed an opportunity to tell him that he was still young and didn't know very much, while the younger hunters were too accustomed to thinking of him as one of their own.

To avoid a confrontation, Au stalked angrily into the forest. The time of the light northern nights was on the wane. The birds, preparing for night, fluttered around in the trees of the forest and then were silent. The smaller forest animals crawled into their holes, but the night hunters came out to stalk their prey. In the lakes, pike swam silently along the very bottoms, while above them slid the dark shadows of otters. A lynx crouched on a fat branch awaiting its prey, while wolves roamed silently through the night. Somewhere in the distance a she-bear called to her scattered cubs. She herself feared no one, but her silly children could perish under the claws of a lynx or in the jaws of a wolf.

His anger at the other hunters was choking him, and Au wandered, not knowing why, farther and farther into the forest. Without having to look under his feet, he walked in the manner of an experienced hunter, so that there wasn't a crack of a broken twig to be heard. At another time, Au would surely have seen the flaming green eyes of a lynx crouched on the branch of a nearby tree, but his mind was on other matters.

Au wandered a long time in the forest, not noticing how the time passed. Usually keenly sensitive to each forest sound and movement, he saw and heard nothing, until he almost stepped on a young thrush. The fledgling was flapping his downy wings, opening his beak as wide as it would go, and squeaking with all his might. But he could not fly. Au bent down over the bird. It was already beginning to be daylight, and he could see that the bird's foot was tangled up in the thick grass and it had not the strength to free itself. Au carefully stretched out his hand to untangle the mass of grass. The little bird hissed angrily and ruffled up all its feathers and pecked at the hunter's fingers. Au burst out laughing—what a brave little bird to attack such an enormous enemy. He freed the bird with some difficulty, for the little one continued its struggle, and placed it on his hand. The bird ruffled up its feathers again and waited to see what would happen next. When Au moved his finger even slightly, the bird quickly gave him another angry peck and flew off.

The incident made Au forget his anger, and he calmly made his way back to the camp. But before he got there he thought to himself, "When necessary, I will continue to do things my own way."

Geese and ducks raised their young in the swamps and lakes hidden in remote corners of the forest. Carefully guarding their offspring from innumerable dangers, the mother birds removed themselves and their children to the little islands that dotted the lakes. Neither man nor beasts of prey made their way to these. The thick growths of sedge along the shoreline hid the weakened molting cocks. Their previously strong wings were now covered with ratty down. During this time the birds could not fly and just ran along the ground, helplessly flapping their naked wings, though they were still at home on the water. Sensing the presence of an enemy, they dove deep, and swam toward the center of the lake, where they would wait out the danger.

The young people hunted for the "molters" in groups. One of them would search out the bird and chase it to where the others lay in wait. That was when the real fun began. The frightened geese hissed loudly, the girls chasing them shrieked at the top of their lungs, and the boys shouted joyfully. The ganders were very clever and tried to scamper into the thick sedge, which cut up the bare legs and feet of the hunters. But the young people's passion for hunting was so strong that they climbed into the very thickest sedge, unafraid of the boggiest place, and if the bird made it into the water they would leap in and swim after it.

This year Tibu decided to go after the birds near a lake with a bad reputation. It was surrounded all around by boggy swamps and its shores were thickly overgrown with reeds and sedge. The swamps blocked access to the lake for people and beasts of prey, so that the birds enjoyed a great expanse of safe ground, and there were many birds. Tibu took a group of the bravest boys and girls with him. Among these was Bright Star, granddaughter of the old koldunya who had died of hunger in the spring. Tibu had gladly taken her along on the hunt, for she was considered the nimblest, fastest duck hunter of all the girls. It was not an accident that her necklace of duckbills from the ducks she herself had caught was the longest of any girl in the village. Tibu was amazed by her boldness, and the girl was flattered that the young man, already initiated into the hunters, was befriending her. Somehow it happened that they found themselves constantly side by side during the hunt.

Picking a little hillock for a campground, Tibu assigned partners for searching expeditions and pointed them in the directions where he thought they would find game. Bright Star was again Tibu's partner.

They headed toward one of the small coves, overgrown very thickly with rushes. The shoreline along here was so swampy that it hadn't dried up even in this very hot period. Bright Star and Tibu found themselves wading through water most of the time, but they knew that this was a particularly good hunting ground. As they approached the rushes, they heard a sound much like coughing, coming from all around them. It was the sound that geese made during this time of year. And although neither the boy nor the girl said a word to each other, they both were thinking the same thing: how to get as many geese as possible. Not in order to brag to their friends but for other reasons. For it was the custom among young people to exchange necklaces of duckbills as a pledge of affection.

This year Bright Star was to acquire a dugout of her own. Tibu also still lived in his mother's dugout. To give a present of a necklace of duckbills was to make a proposal. The necklaces were given by the young women as well as the young men, and there was nothing unusual in a girl's presenting a necklace to the young man of her choice.

Geese have very sensitive hearing, and to approach their nests Tibu and Bright Star had to pass through the rustling reeds. Although the wind helped them today, the going had to be very slow. When a little gust of wind rustled up the reeds, they moved a few steps forward, and when the wind died down they stayed very still.

It became difficult for two people to pass through the thick growth together and Bright Star and Tibu separated. After a time Bright Star caught sight of a goose, headed in the direction of the lake, and not wanting the goose to disappear underwater, she made a quick lunge after it. But as she jumped she felt herself falling right through the undergrowth into a deep icy quagmire. Her legs were buried and her body rested on a thickly tangled net of roots and water plants. Slowly these roots were separating and sinking under the weight of her body.

Bright Star screamed for help, but the thick growth of sedge rustled indifferently over her head and it seemed to her that her cries got tangled up in its thickness and went no further. She felt her unsteady support giving way beneath her. Would Tibu hear her cries? Would he be able to tell where the cries were coming from? Would he reach her in time? Again and again the girl called to her friend. The water was rising higher and higher and her legs grew numb. She managed to turn over carefully on her back, and she lay on a new place where the net of roots was a little stronger. But soon the water started to rise around her again. . . . Would Tibu never come?

As time wore on, Bright Star began to despair and her cries grew weak. Let whatever will be, be, she thought.

But when the swampy water reached the top of her chest, she became so frightened that she found reserves of strength previously unknown to her, and she managed to move to another place again.

Tibu had heard her cries, but had lost precious minutes searching frantically for their source. Finally arriving, he picked up three long poles and laying himself down across these poles he grabbed the girl by the hands. Very carefully, slowly, and gradually he pulled her to him.

Neither one of them knew how much time passed in this fight for life, but in time the swamp released its grip on the girl's legs. And at last both were on firm ground once more. The girl began to dry her mud-soaked clothing, and as the hot sun warmed her, her shivering subsided.

When Tibu and Bright Star returned that evening to the campground on the hillock, they, and their companions, knew clearly that when Bright Star possessed her own dugout, no one but Tibu would share it with her.

Chapter 18

THE HERRING had left the shores of the White Sea long ago, and the larger sea animals—seals, walrus, whales—had gone with them. In search of food, they had moved to the Sun and Moon, for that is what the hunters called the two islands, one small and one large, that rose out of the sea at a distance of a day's travel from the shore. Here in the deep straits around the islands the smaller fish gathered, as well as the larger fish that fed on them. No matter from what direction the wind came, the fish and sea animals could always find shelter from the storm in the narrow straits and winding bays.

Each fall, hunters came here to catch the walrus and seal. This was a dangerous and dreary enterprise. For days the lead-colored waves slapped lazily against the sides of the boats and then suddenly out of nowhere a wind would spring up, and instantly the boats were surrounded by enormous billows topped with whitecaps. Woe then to hunters who have ventured out to sea! One moment's tardiness in turning the boat across the wave, and instantly the enormous wall of water would overturn the boat. Many, very many, hunters had perished hunting by these islands.

But the younger hunters did not go to the islands, for this was also the time of the deer hunt. And while the Glavni led the older men after walrus and seal, the younger men chased deer in the forest.

Twice now small storms had come from the sea, harbingers of autumn. The older hunters began to prepare for the sea voyage: patching the boats, sharpening harpoons, cutting leather ropes from the kneaded skins. The sea hunt was different from hunting in the forest. A wounded animal in the forest is easily tracked, but, in the water, finding and hitting the animal is only the first step in the hunt. How many wounded whales, seals, and walruses had disappeared in the watery depths, taking precious weapons with them.

The shaman also had to prepare for the hunt. He went to the Sacred Cliff and began to chisel on its face the images of the animals that each hunter wanted to kill at the hunt. He was so engrossed in his task that he didn't notice Au's appearance at his side.

"I do not wish to go on the sea hunt," Au said. "That is work for old men—lying on one's stomach for days waiting until a stupid walrus shows himself. I want to chase deer in the forest as I have in previous years. I want to run faster than the deer themselves. I have tried to talk to the old men about this, but they know only one thing, 'The Glavni belongs on the sea hunt!' Well, Kremen was an old man, he could not hunt after deer, but I can!"

Liok thought about it. There was not, he argued, a better hunter than Au in the village. But what could he do about the old men? They never willingly accepted a departure from tradition.

"I will help you," he told his friend. "Come here this evening." When Au appeared again that evening, Liok reached into his vest and pulled out two small brown roots.

"Eat these. They will make you sick and the old men will not want you to go with them, for fear the spirit of the sickness will enter them too."

Au took the roots, thought for a moment, and shook his head. "No, I cannot do that. How can I lie to my own men?" he said and tossed the roots into the rapids.

"And if the older hunters agree that you may not stay behind, will you go?"

"No! I will not go. I am the Glavni and they cannot give me orders." Au's eyes sparkled angrily. "I have already killed a whale and I will kill many deer in the forest. Do you remember how many antlers I brought back last year?"

The season had come to set out on the journey. But the day had not been set because the omens had been poor. Either the sun set in a cloud, or the moon was too red. Finally, the moon shone silver in a clear sky and the calm flight of gulls showed that there would be no storms. The next day they would set out to sea.

That evening, Au entered the large dugout of The Bearded Old Man and announced to the hunters that he was staying to hunt deer.

"Why do you, Glavni, break the traditions of the people?" the old men argued. "Would Kremen ever have sent us off alone?"

"He was an old man," answered Au, "he could never catch the deer which run swift as the wind. But why should I lie on my belly in a boat, when my legs can run fast?"

The young hunters who had accompanied Au loudly supported him. But the old men were not swayed, and old Niuk argued vehemently.

"You are veteran hunters, experienced and without equal on the sea," Au said soothingly. "Wouldn't it be better for you to follow old Niuk, who killed his first 'white worm' before I was even born?"

The old men could not disagree with this. Niuk did know a great deal about the habits of sea animals, for he had hunted them for more years than even they could remember. Thus it was settled. The next morning the older hunters left for the sea, without Au.

Chapter 19

SOON AFTER THE DEPARTURE of the old hunters, the younger ones left for the forest. The time had passed when the deer spent entire days standing in the lakes, only their nostrils showing above the water, to escape from the gadflies. In the fall the flies disappeared and the deer could roam the forest freely. Their fur grew shiny and they grew fatter and lazier.

Gathering the hunters around him, Au gave instructions on where to look for deer and sent them off in different directions so that, in chasing after the deer, their paths would not cross.

Au took Bei as his helper. The day he had chosen for the hunt was gray and cloudy. Branches and undergrowth did not make as much noise underfoot on damp ground, and the wind gusting through the leaves filled the air with an endless rustling noise. On a day like this the deer were not as keen-eared as usual and not as watchful.

The javelin was the favorite weapon of the younger hunters. From a short distance it killed a deer instantly, one needed only a strong arm. Older hunters preferred a bow and arrow—an arrow flew a much longer distance than a javelin and they didn't have to stalk as close. The argument about which weapon was superior continued from generation to generation. But Au and Bei had no disagreements. Both were young and strong and the javelin was their best friend.

Picking edible mushrooms along the way, they walked side by side in search of tracks, never taking their eyes from the damp ground. During the search for game all conversation was forbidden, even in whispers. Suddenly Au stopped in his tracks. Bei also froze, although he could not see what had come to Au's attention. Then looking in the same direction as his friend he understood immediately. On the ground were some deer droppings. Both hunters dropped down on all fours. Their keen eyes saw the faint traces of the divided deer hoof. A large, older buck had passed by here this morning. In the fall the animals became lazy and did not travel long distances, so they could expect him to be somewhere nearby. A good hunter never loses a track once he has found it, and Au was a good hunter. Slowly, carefully they moved forward, stopping every once in a while, touching each other to point out some mark left by an animal. It was evident that the deer had been walking slowly and calmly from one patch of mushrooms to another. The naked mushroom stems sticking up from the ground showed his path.

The sun was getting ready to set when the hunters sighted the ambling deer in a meadow through some trees. A cold chill ran down Bei's spine. He looked pleadingly at Au. "Let me throw first," his eyes were begging. But although Au would have gladly given his life for his friend, he could not put aside his right to deliver the first blow.

Dropping to one knee and clutching the javelin in his hand he waited until the deer turned sideways. The javelin whistled through the air and lodged itself in the deer's belly.

The buck swayed unsteadily and raised himself up on his hind legs.

"Throw!" shouted Au to Bei. Bei's javelin, aimed at the neck, hit the antlers and glanced off. The buck fell forward onto his knees, but immediately leaped up and raced forward. He ran blindly, head down and antlers pitched forward. Without breaking his run, Au picked up Bei's javelin and examined it. The sharp flint point had broken in half from the impact against the antlers. Soon Au's javelin also dislodged itself from the animal's side. Bei wanted to throw it after the fleeing animal, but Au grabbed it out of his hand. To lend someone else one's weapon during the hunt was bad luck for the owner.

As they gave chase, the forest thinned out and opened onto a large dry swamp covered with rust red moss. The experienced old buck knew well that he must avoid this place. His sharp hoofs would stick in the soft water-soaked moss, and he would never get away. He turned sharply and began to run around the edge of the swamp, which was strewn with enormous boulders. With a new burst of energy the hunters raced after him, for there was not a second to lose. They could easily lose all traces of the wounded animal in this boulder-strewn place. But the buck made several desperate leaps and disappeared behind a large rock. When Bei and Au came around the rock, the buck was nowhere in sight.

The hunters looked around but all they could see were rocks and cliffs. Not only were there no hoofprints on the rocky ground, but no trace of blood could be seen. Au ordered Bei to run straight ahead, and he himself ran to the left. He wandered for a long time among the boulders, until he heard nearby the sound of labored breathing. Holding his javelin in readiness, the hunter stole silently toward the sound. But the buck, weakened by the loss of blood, was already dying.

Au loudly called to Bei, and by the time he arrived the buck was dead. According to hunting custom, a dead animal belonged to all who had hunted it, but only the hunter who had dealt the death blow received the strip of skin around the neck of the buck. This was covered with long silvery hairs and was considered the finest adornment for a woman's dress clothes. Thus, the more successful the hunter, the better dressed was the woman in whose dugout he lived.

Helping Au skin the deer, Bei watched enviously as Au carefully cut off the valuable neckpiece. Au noted this and was about to cut the piece in half, but realized that it would be ruined as an ornament and would not bring joy to either one of them. Then he removed from around his own neck a necklace of wolf fangs and handed it to his friend.

Bei's face shone with happiness. This was the best present of all. Along with the teeth taken from the wolves killed by Au himself, a part of Au's strength and hunter's luck was given with the gift.

The day's hunt had begun successfully. The hunters had come back with four deer and one fawn. Tired but pleased, they carried the heavy skinned carcasses back to the village.

"It is clear that Roko loves Au," they whispered among themselves on the way back, pleased that he had remained with them.

But their kinsmen, still at sea, were not speaking of the Glavni so kindly. Tradition had been broken, and the hunters feared that the hunt would go badly. Yet, as if in spite of their grumbling, they had good wind the entire way and the boats quickly reached their destination.

In the waters surrounding the islands and in the bays between them, the white whales showed their rounded heads between the waves. The old men recovered their spirits; perhaps the hunt would go well after all. The first day on the big island was devoted to gathering brush and driftwood and building fires to drive out any evil spirits who might have settled in the abandoned campground while they were away.

While gathering driftwood on the rocky beach, Niuk found a piece of an oar, covered with intricate carvings. He looked it over for a long time with his old eyes, which could see things well in the distance yet not so well close up, and shook his head approvingly—the carvings were made by able hands. Then suddenly he remembered that many many years ago he himself had carved that very sun, so that it would not set throughout the hunt, those very whales, so that they would attract real whales, and that same boat filled with hunters sailing peacefully on a calm sea. He had given this oar to his friend Tyaku, but it had not brought luck. That very spring, a whale wounded by Tyaku's harpoon had turned over the boat he was in and Niuk's friend had drowned.

All that evening Niuk remembered the old days and his friend. That night he dreamed about Tyaku and in the dream Tyaku said nothing, he just stood leaning on the oar and then disappeared. In the morning, when the hunters were eating smoked salmon around the fire, Niuk told his dream to them. "He wanted to say something, and was afraid to say it," said the old man. "It's bad, very bad. I think he was trying to give some warning about trouble at sea."

The other hunters caught Niuk's anxiety, and they debated for a long time whether it was wise to go out to sea or not, then decided that it would be better to wait for another day.

The whales played in the waters around them as if to taunt them, but the hunters sat around the shore, each telling one frightening tale after another. Many of the older ones remembered Tyaku well. One of them had almost drowned with him, but had grabbed hold of the overturned boat just in time. But Tyaku had been tossed aside by a wave and, since like all his people he did not know how to swim, he quickly drowned.

That night three more hunters saw Tyaku in their dreams. One of them was told by Tyaku to hunt for walruses, but these walruses ran around on the land instead of swimming in the water; another dreamed how he was sailing in a boat with Tyaku and suddenly in the middle of calm water the boat overturned. But the dream that frightened the hunters most was the third one; Tyaku told the dreamer that they must leave the islands as quickly as possible, for the spirits were angry and were planning to drown them all.

In the morning they debated about why the spirits would be so angry with them. Might it not be that the Glavni had broken with tradition? Then they decided that they had best return to the village before trouble overtook them. And they immediately put out the fires, got into the boats, and sailed home without a single kill.

Chapter 20

THERE WERE STILL many days left before the hunters could finish their work and return for the winter to the dugouts of the village. The women, however, were already gathering and storing firewood, changing the poles supporting the walls of the dugouts, and evening out the floors. Some of them were sewing bits of brightly colored furs onto their clothing so as to look more festive.

Before the return of the hunters, three young women had to leave the dugouts of their mothers and obtain dugouts of their own. The move into her own dugout was as important an event in a girl's life as the initiation of hunters was for a young man.

On the first sunny day after a full moon, a group of noisy young people gathered outside the dugout of Red Fox, Bright Star's mother. Bright Star was to have the first new dugout. Soon the High Koldunya appeared with her entourage. She entered the dugout where Red Fox and Bright Star were sitting by the hearth. The old woman took the young girl by the hand and led her out to the anxiously awaiting crowd. As was the custom, her mother remained sitting at her hearth.

Once, many years before, hunters used to come from

other villages and lead the girls of their choice away to new homes. But since the time of the great plague when all the neighboring villages had died out, the solemn procession of the young girls away from their native village was replaced by the ritual of choosing a site for the new dugout. Accompanied by the koldunyii and by the friends of her childhood, the young girl walked around the outskirts of the village, until she stumbled against a stone or her foot tripped in a pothole. That place became the site of the new dugout.

Bright Star walked slowly around the village, behind her the old koldunyii watched her feet carefully, and behind them the crowd of her friends followed. Sticking their heads outside their dugouts, the women of the village called their good wishes and congratulations to her: that the hunter who settled in her dugout be brave and strong, that there always be enough to eat in her dugout, that the happy cries of newborn children make themselves heard as soon as possible, and that sickness never find its way to her door.

Bright Star did not wander around the village for too long. She had a long time ago found a favored place near the edge of the forest by four large birch trees growing in a row. A few days ago she had secretly brought a large stone there and as she passed by now, she purposely caught her foot on it. The High Koldunya cried immediately, "Here! Here is where it will be."

Her friends quickly ran to the place where they had previously laid firewood in store and, gathering large armfuls, carried the sticks and branches to the site of the new dugout. Soon a large heap of firewood lay in a pile under the birches, whose brightly yellow leaves rustled musically in the wind. Bright Star brought fire from her mother's dugout and lit the wood. The fire was necessary to cleanse the area of evil spirits.

While the flames burned brightly and the firewood crackled, the young people discussed all the details of the upcoming job—for the dugout had to last for many years. The discussions were still going on when Tibu arrived out of breath. Everyone had already guessed that Tibu and no one else would be sharing the dugout with Bright Star, and Au had released him from his duties for the day to build the dugout. Tibu cast a masterful glance at the assembled materials and workers and began giving orders. First he asked the two tallest youths to lie down on the ground, the tops of their heads touching, and with a sharp stone he made a mark on the ground by their feet. That was to be the length of the dugout. Then he himself lay down crosswise to that line and someone else marked off the place where his outstretched fingertips reached and where his toes were. Using these marks as guidelines he drew a rough oval connecting them. Now the digging could begin.

Everyone worked willingly and with high spirits. The young men used sticks with pointed ends to loosen the ground and the girls, using scoops made of birchwood, shoveled out the earth within the lines that Tibu had drawn.

The hole deepened quickly and the pile of dirt from it grew just as quickly. Tibu shouted encouragement to his friends, for he wanted the hole to be a deep one. In a shallow dugout the smoke from the hearth would spread low on the ground making its inhabitants cry even when they were happy. The hole would be deep enough when Bright Star, standing in the middle of the dugout, could not reach a wooden pole placed across the top.

Then the girls began to pound down the earthen floor, which sloped gently down from the entrance of the dugout toward the center. They flattened down each bump and filled each depression, treading down the earth with their dancing feet. Then a hollow was scooped out in the center of the dugout for the hearth, and two smaller ones were dug by the entranceway for the clay waterpots. The men, in the meantime, were evening out the earthen walls and installing the wooden poles that would support the roof. The spaces between the poles were plastered with clay that had been mixed with wet sand. The supporting poles were fastened on the tops and bottoms with well-tarred cross poles.

Working quickly, Tibu tried to hurry his companions along, while Bright Star kept looking anxiously at the sky —the time allotted to build a dugout was between sunrise and sunset. If the sun set before a fire blazed in the hearth of the new dugout, then the dugout had to be left unfinished and a new one could not be built until the following year.

The roofing was the most difficult part. It had to be waterproof and sturdy enough to support the heavy layer of snow that would soon cover it. First, carefully cut poles were laid across the walls. Then several layers of birch bark were added as covering. A layer of sand went over this, followed by wet clay. Finally the roof was covered with layers of fresh turf, so that in the spring the roof was covered with a carpet of green grass.

The dugout was finished long before sunset. And although it differed not at all from the neighboring dugouts, the young couple were sure that they had the best dwelling in the village. It was not large, but several people could sit inside comfortably around the hearth, and in the back four or five people could sleep comfortably.

The koldunyii now chased away all the young people eagerly crowding around the doorway. It was their turn to perform their duties. The first task was to build the hearth. Whispering incantations, the old women covered the hole with clay, then they poured in sand and laid out the stones.

The High Koldunya and one helper hung a curtain made of two deerskins over the doorway, with the fur lining facing inside. To keep illness from the dugout, she took a lynx paw out of her pouch and buried it in front of the entrance. Several roots and herbs were buried right next to it.

And then it was time to make the fire, and Bright Star's mother was called. Red Fox brought with her a clay pot containing hot coals from her own fire. By the light of the new fire in the dugout, the old woman intoned the necessary incantations over the new mistress of the house. Then Bright Star was left alone in her new dwelling, bare as it was. No thick skins would warm her sleep, for the bedding of the household must be supplied by the hunter who was to live there; and the hunters were still living in their camp. Tibu dare not appear with his wedding gifts yet. Bright Star would sleep as best she could on the bare floor, curled up close to the hearth.

Chapter 21

BRIGHT STAR was not alone in her dugout for long. As the autumn rains came, the hunters left their camp and returned to live in the village. The fire in the hearth seemed to burn more brightly and the dry wood crackled more gaily when Tibu, carrying an enormous bundle of animal furs and skins, entered Bright Star's dugout.

The other dugouts were happier and livelier as well. The women had cooked meat and fish all day long for the welcoming of the men. They had saved up large stores over the summer and food was plentiful. The time for rest had come, and they lay on their soft furs by the fires and ate and slept.

Only the shaman was lonely and bored at this time. In order to pass the long, dark autumn days more quickly, he carved a bone amulet to replace the figure of the man that he had lost, and the new figure came out even better than the old one. The lost man had had a round flat head and the arms were just lines drawn on the body. The figurine that Liok had carved had a shaman's hat on its head, and its hands held a drum.

The cold rains gradually changed to frosts, and the

autumn winds blew off the last faded leaves from the trees. The sky became crowded with low winter clouds; the stinging snow whirled in blizzards. Then the winds died down and the slow, quiet snowfalls began. Heavy white hats perched shakily on the lowered branches of the fir trees.

The pliant birches and aspens doubled over from the weight of the snow and were, at last, covered over completely. The northern winter had come.

The winter hunting season began with the hunt for elk. As soon as the ground was completely covered with snow, Au and Bei went on snowshoes into the forest. Toward midday, they happened on a path of many elk prints leading to a waterhole. Au found a comfortable lookout behind a row of low pine trees that lined the path. The very next day, he brought his hunters there.

Choosing trees with thick, strong trunks, the hunters built small platforms in the branches. When they were finished, two hunters climbed onto each platform. The thick branches concealed the hunters well, and they rubbed their clothes with fresh turf to keep the animals from detecting their scent.

The forest was as quiet as only a forest on a windless winter day can be, when not a branch is moving. Only occasionally could be heard the hollow rumble of snowcaps here and there as they fell off the branches of the trees.

Liok lay in a hunting blind beside Au, when a mass of snow fell loudly from a nearby spruce. Au happily whispered to Liok, "Roko is giving us a sign that he sends a herd of elk." But quite some time still had to pass before they saw the lower branches of the pines sway as the herd appeared on the path. In the lead was an old buck, right behind him was a large female and beside her, sometimes straying behind and sometimes running forward, was a young calf. A little way behind were two more females with their young.

Up to now Liok had seen elk only from a distance. Their sense of smell is very sensitive and they do not allow men to come up close to them. But now the old buck was walking with an even step, wearily shaking his head, which was weighted down with enormous antlers. Before reaching the pines that hid the hunters, he stopped suddenly and sharply drew in his breath, smelling the air all around him.

The buck stood for some time, hesitating, carefully gazing all around; the females obediently frozen in their tracks. Finally the leader lowered his ears and slowly moved forward. When he was even with the pine which concealed Au, the Glavni threw his spear. The elk snorted and leaped to the side. The calf walking beside the first female fell with pitiful cries. The female clumsily reared back, and Tibu's spear just grazed her smooth fur. Bellowing with fright, the other calves raced after their mothers, as they disappeared into the forest.

The old buck made two, three, steps and stopped, the spear wobbling back and forth in his side. Mortally wounded, his whole body shaking, he slowly raised up his head, snorting fiercely and ready to face his enemy. But everything around him was still; the hunters remained hidden in their perches in the pines. A stream of blood flowed from his wound, and created red patterns in the white snow. He weakened quickly from the loss of blood and his heavy head lowered to the ground. Once more he raised his head, swayed from side to side, and to keep himself from falling widened the stance of his legs. But his knees were shaking more and more, and finally his head fell for the last time.

The hunters jumped down from their perches with joyous

cries. Seeing the people, the buck tried to raise his head again, but didn't have the strength, and with a short bellow of pain and rage he tumbled onto his side.

The warm blood of freshly killed game was the favorite delicacy of the hunters. They pierced a vein in the buck's neck and taking turns, older hunters first, they drank the blood. The younger hunters only got to scoop up the salty red snow. But when Liok took up a handful of this snow, old Niuk angrily shouted at him to leave off. "You must go at once," he said to the shaman, "we must make our peace with the elk. The uninitiated cannot watch."

Liok left the hunters sadly. Making for the Sacred Cliff he reached for his chisel, and slowly, dot by dot, a huge elk appeared on the red granite, with enormous antlers, and a spear sticking out of his side.

Chapter 22

HAVING MISSED the autumn hunt, the village was without the thick strong skins of the walrus from which to make waterproof footwear and clothing. They were without the blubber that they used to rub on their faces and hands so the skin wouldn't crack in the cold wind and frost. And so, because of the fear of the old men, it was necessary to undertake a more difficult and dangerous winter hunt.

The shaman was always taken along on the more dangerous hunts, in the hope that his spirits would bring luck. So once again, Liok accompanied the hunters to the familiar sanctuary in the cliffs where the hunting clothes were stored. He had not been there since the terrible morning when to save his friend he had deceived his people. The hunters, too, had stayed away fearing Bloody Khoro. But they could not hunt the Bearded Old Man without their gear.

Once dressed, they moved toward the sea. On the beach between the cliffs they found their boats scattered around by a recent blizzard.

It was a cloudy windless morning. The sky was gray, and only in the east where it met the water was there a strip of clear blue sky. Slowly the great waves rolled over one another. They too were dark gray and only their crests rising high into the air reflected a greenish tinge.

The boats separated. Liok sat in the stern of his boat as it sailed along the icy shoreline. He watched as the other two boats slowly disappeared in the opposite direction. In the same boat with him were Bei, old Niuk, and Tibu. For Liok, as for Tibu, this was the first walrus hunt, and both youths sat craning their necks in every direction.

They sailed for a long time along the icy edge of the shore, barely able to make out the hazy spot that was the sun in the whitish twilight which hung over the sea.

Liok wanted desperately to be the first one to catch sight of a walrus, but he was unlucky. The very instant he rubbed his weary eyes, the hunters sighted a walrus hidden behind a mound of ice.

Bei and Tibu carefully swung their oars and turned the boats sharply in toward the shore. A short low bellow like that of a bear sounded from behind the ice. Niuk climbed quickly and silently out onto the ice, carrying a harpoon with a long sharp point in his right hand. A strong thin leather rope was tied to the harpoon, and the other end of the rope was tied to a wooden block on the bottom of the boat. As Niuk crawled toward the walrus, Bei carefully watched the older hunter's every move, slowly uncoiling the rope, while Tibu, leaning an oar against the ice, kept the boat motionless.

From behind the ice they heard a loud sigh followed by noisy stirrings. Niuk crawled faster and soon disappeared behind a hill of ice.

Once more they heard a bellow from the Bearded Old Man, only this time it was not short and sleepy, but rather long and threatening. A large round head with tusks and long whiskers emerged from behind the hummock of ice.

Slapping his fins loudly, the huge animal was clumsily making his way to the water. As if blind with pain, he was headed right for the boat. Bei pushed the boat out of his way, and the hulking beast fell into the sea with a great splash. Not a second later Bei flung out the remainder of the coiled rope and the wooden block.

Old Niuk ran to the edge of the ice but did not jump into the boat. With his hands raised above his eyes, he and the others looked out over the water. Neither the walrus nor the float could be seen on the waves. If the animal had crawled under the ice, they could say good-bye to their catch as well as the harpoon, leather rope, and float. They heaved a sigh of relief when they spied the float among the waves, and a little beyond it the walrus's round head. The animal was seriously wounded, and the water around it darkened with blood. The walrus dove and reappeared again, but they could see that he was growing weaker. Bei and Tibu brought the boat alongside the wooden block as it bobbed in the waves. They lifted it into the boat and, returning to the edge of the ice, threw it to Niuk, who had remained there. The old man tied the rope several times around a large rock. He and Bei, who was out of the boat by now, began to haul in the line. They pulled with all their combined strength until, after many suspenseful moments, the now exhausted body of the walrus came into view just a few yards from the edge of the ice.

Niuk carefully made a loop in the rope and skillfully threw it around the animal. They could not afford to waste a second, for if the walrus died, his lungs would immediately fill with water, and he would sink like a stone to the bottom of the sea. Using his oar Bei brought in a flat chunk of floating ice and, jumping onto it, made his way over to the animal. Throwing another loop around the walrus's front fins, he managed to maneuver the piece of ice right under the walrus's body. The little iceberg bobbled wildly, and Bei almost lost his footing, but it straightened out and the now-dead walrus was pulled up onto shore.

As they ripped open the belly of the Bearded Old Man, the stench from the bloody, steaming innards was so strong that even the seasoned hunters had to turn away their faces. Liok was happy to leave when Niuk ordered him to make a fire on the shore so that the other hunters could see from the smoke that they should come in. The shaman gathered the driftwood that had been brought ashore in the autumn storms and made a fire.

Seeing the signal, the hunters in the other boats turned and came quickly to shore.

Liok could see from a distance that Niuk had taken out the skin of an unborn deer and, holding it before him, was bowing first in the direction of the dead walrus and then to the sea. He was performing the peacemaking ritual.

Heavy snow clouds covered the sky and it grew dark before evening time. The walrus was tied up with ropes and dragged to firmer ground. Then they returned for the boats and dragged these inland. It was now quite dark, and large flakes of snow fell on the hunters.

Chapter 23

NEARBY, at the very edge of the forest, there stood an outpost—a dugout that had been erected a very long time ago, specifically for those who found themselves having to spend the night here.

They dragged the walrus close to the fire and gathered enough firewood to burn all night. Niuk remained to guard the dead animal. Groaning, he lowered himself on a bundle of wood right next to the fire.

Au led the hunters to the dugout. The fire blazed brightly, outlining a reddish yellow circle in the snow, and within this circle he could see the huddled-up figure of old Niuk. Au knew what it meant to spend a freezing night by the fire. If you got too close, your face and clothing burned; if you moved away, then the cold got into your very bones. In the crowded little dugout, however, the hunters all lay down together, each hunter pressing his chest against another man's back, and soon they were all as warm as they would be under the furs in their own dugouts. Au pitied the old man. A freezing, sleepless night would be hard on him. The Glavni stopped and let the other hunters pass him. When the last had gone by, Au went back to the fire.

"Go on to the dugout," he told Niuk, "I will stay here."

Niuk's old body was aching so badly, and the thought of the warm dugout was so tempting, that he silently got up and, taking his spear, left to join the other hunters, while Au remained to guard the walrus.

In the summer, one can always tell by the reddening glow at the edge of the sky how soon the sun will rise. In the winter, the night seems endless. And so it seemed now to the young hunter sitting by the fire. Adding wood very sparingly, Au thought sadly, "The spirits who put the cap of darkness on the earth each day must have fallen fast asleep and forgotten to take it off."

The billows of acrid smoke burned his eyes, and his clothing, all damp from the night, seemed to cut into his shoulders. Au tried stretching out on the carcass of the walrus, but his teeth started chattering from the cold. Once again he moved closer to the fire, and again the smoke burned his eyes.

But Au was not alone in that freezing night. Not far from him, an old bear lumbered out of the forest onto the icy beach, hidden in the darkness of the night. All the other bears had long since gone into hibernation. This bear too had burrowed away for the winter, but a younger bear had driven him off and taken over his lair, by right of the eternal laws of nature.

The older bear had not given up easily and had suffered badly in the fight. His fur hung in clumps around exposed wounds, and the frost intensified the pain. He was fated to a hungry death, but bears have great endurance and few die easily. This bear had not eaten for many days and wandered across the snow, ravenous with hunger. Now, his sensitive nose had caught the smell of walrus meat. Now he no longer wobbled with weakness; he forgot about the pain in his wounds and he gathered what remained of his previous strength.

But the bear had to face a man and had not caught Au unaware. Au caught the smell of the stinking wounds and the rotting fur. Stepping behind the fire he stood with his spear pointing before him, the wooden end of it stuck in the ground by his foot for support. The enormous hulk of bear jumped right over the fire. The point of the spear ripped through the bear's belly and emerged on the other side. But the wooden end of the spear could not bear the weight and broke like a twig. The terrible weight of the bear descended on Au and crushed out his life. With no one to add wood, the fire slowly burnt itself out, leaving the body of poor Au and the dying bear in the cold.

Old people sleep less than young ones. In the middle of the night Niuk woke up and could sleep no more. The thought that he had not remained to guard his catch worried the hunter. As much as he wanted to lie in the warmth, as frightful as the cold outside was, Niuk made himself get up.

It was very crowded in the dugout; there was nowhere even to put a foot down. The old man crawled across the sleeping hunters to the doorway.

Leaning on his spear for support, he walked toward the beach trying not to stray from the path the hunters had made in the snow. On reaching the turn beyond which lay the beach, Niuk stopped in his tracks. Nowhere could he see the glow of a fire. "Au has fallen asleep and let the fire go out!" thought Niuk in horror. "How could the Glavni ever be forgiven such a sin? Now the evil spirits will surely bring bad times."

By the laws of the village, a hunter who fell asleep while guarding a fire faced severe punishment. The old hunter was stricken with horror and indecision. For it was he and not Au who should have been spending the night keeping vigil over the carcass of the walrus and the fire. The young hunter had pitied him and tried to help. But the gratitude he felt toward Au was not as strong as the anger. The Glavni's guilt was too great—because of him, the entire village, he thought, was now threatened with disaster.

Niuk returned to the dugout and woke the hunters. He told them that Au had evidently fallen asleep and let the fire go out. The wind had probably scattered the ashes by now and they would have to start the fire all over again.

Only as they came right up to the dead ashes of the fire did they realize what had happened.

The bear was still alive, but so weak that he made no attempt to get up and only raised his head slightly when he smelled the hunters. With a short bellow he dropped his head onto the carcass of the walrus.

The hunters did not even see Au right away. The great body of the bear covered him completely and only one foot stuck out.

Spears pierced the bear's body from all sides. He bellowed again, tried to raise himself up on his front paws, and fell over heavily onto his back. Now everyone saw Au's head, his hideously twisted arm. Bei and Liok rushed to their friend.

A silence more painful than cries and wails gripped the hunters for a long time. Niuk, who had remained alive because Au had decided to sit in his place through the frosty night; Bei, for whom Au was a teacher and dearest friend; Liok, who had placed so many hopes on the new Glavni; and all the other hunters, stood silently and could not tear their eyes away from their dead companion. Finally, barely able to utter the words, Niuk said, "Light the fire!"

When the fire was burning brightly once again, the hunters dragged the dead bear to the side. The animal had not disfigured Au. Neither his teeth nor his claws had touched the young hunter.

Au's spear was still stuck in the bear's side, and although the wooden end had broken in half, the spearhead, which had passed through the bear without encountering a bone, was whole. Old Niuk pulled the spearhead out of the animal and said, "This is mine!" To take the weapon of the dead Glavni was to take his place. No one argued with Niuk. They all agreed.

A hunter must be buried where he meets his death. But since the ground was frozen solid, the hunters decided to cover Au's body with stones. They cut off the bear's head and paws and laid them with Au's body, then covered all with branches. They gathered stones, which had to be dug out of the snow, and the burial mound grew slowly.

When the body was completely covered, they drove a long pole into the ground and placed the bear's head on top of it. Let it be pecked by birds and drenched by rain, let it freeze in the winter and suffer from thirst under the hot summer sun. Other bears living in the forest would suffer the same agonies, as a punishment because one of their kin had killed a man.

During the ritual of the burial, all the orders were given by old Niuk. The old man knew all the old customs very well and the dead ancestors had no grievances against him, for he had not broken or forgotten any part of the ritual. The hunters followed his orders unquestioningly, for they knew that all would be well for Au in his new life if they observed all the rituals properly.

Having finished the rites, they took the boats to the water and returned home. And Niuk sat in the place of the Glavni.

Chapter 24

THE PEOPLE of the village had learned from early childhood to watch the sun carefully. By looking to see where it was in the sky they could tell the time of day, could find their way in the forest. Even little children knew that when the sun rose from behind the pine with the split top and set behind the enormous shaggy spruce on the hillside the shortest days in the year had set in. After three or four nights, the sun would start to appear more to the left of the pine and to set more and more to the right of the ancient spruce.

From time immemorial, these short days were considered the most dangerous time of the year. The koldunyii told stories that they themselves had heard as girls from the old women, how at this time evil spirits warred with good spirits, and the sun battled with darkness. Who didn't know that the sun gave warmth and sent food? And who didn't know that the darkness gave birth to the twins of cold and hunger? So that the sun would win its battles with the darkness, the people helped it by lighting huge fires at night, which gave light and warmth like the sun, and like the sun kept away evil spirits.

The women and children had been gathering wood for a long time and laying it in large piles around the village in preparation. Back in the autumn, they had pulled out of the river trees and logs that had floated on it, and now they added these to the piles. Finally all was in readiness. Now they waited for the word from the High Koldunya to begin the festival of "Helping the Sun."

The new High Koldunya was not as wise as Fox Paw. Fox Paw had known all the signs as well as the best hunter. Every year, at the onset of the shortest days, Fox Paw had come on starry nights to the pine with the divided top and, always standing in the same place, by the thickest root, she had stared for a long time into the sky. The old woman had carved notches into the pine and scratched mysterious symbols on her rowan stick.

Fox Paw had known much. Like the hunters, she could guess from the sound of a woodpecker's tap what the weather would be the next day. Often she would sit on her haunches and, looking at the snow, could tell from its texture if spring was at hand or, conversely, if there was to be another cold spell. The hunters out hunting would come across the hunched-over woman on the shores of the sea as well as in the thickest forest. The old Koldunya had wandered everywhere, leaning on her staff and watching and listening to everything that went on in the forest and on the sea. Kremen himself had come to her for advice about when and where to start hunting.

On the eve of the festival To Help the Sun, the hunters had always gathered at Fox Paw's dugout, and she predicted to them what the hunting would be like in the new year and of what dangers they should beware.

Fox Paw was no more. The koldunyii who replaced her one by one had neither her knowledge nor her wisdom. When the hunters asked them anything, instead of answering, they would start to complain that Liok had robbed them of their Sacred Cliff and now they had nowhere to talk with their spirits. And what could they know if they could not speak with their spirits?

When the High Koldunya declared that it was time to light the fires, old Niuk came to Liok and said, "The Koldunya says that since you are now the guardian of the Sacred Cliff, you must find out from the spirits what awaits us in the new year. Ask your spirits and tell us what they say this evening."

As long as Au had been the Glavni, no one had asked Liok to speak with the spirits, and he had not needed to pretend and tell lies. Liok wanted to shout out to Niuk that he had never seen or heard from any spirits, that they never visited with him no matter how often he called them. He wanted to shout that he was tired of being a shaman and lying to his people all the time. But he remained silent. How could he ever admit that? The penalty for lying to his kinsmen meant not only death for himself but for his brothers as well.

The young shaman went to his dugout, threw himself down on the pile of animal skins, and lay motionless for a long time, unwillingly listening to the merry voices of the children and adolescents who were piling spruce twigs on top of the wood piles, so that when the fires were lit there would be many sparks.

Once more Liok had to invent something supposedly told to him by the spirits whom he had never seen nor heard from. Shivering from head to toe, Liok crawled between the skins and, warming up in a while, fell quietly asleep. Terrible dreams assailed him and he moaned and tossed around, seemingly asking someone for mercy. Toward the evening he was waked by a voice calling him to come outside.

He found it difficult to wake up after the heavy sleep and staggered as he made his way to the doorway. Stepping outside he squinted for a long time as he realized that the gloomy gray day had come to an end and it was dusk. Heavy clouds filled the sky and tiny snowflakes fell silently to the ground. In front of his dugout sat the hunters, and in front of them stood Niuk.

"What have the spirits told you?" asked the Glavni looking anxiously into the shaman's face. "What will the year be like?"

Liok was struck dumb—he had slept through the time he had been given to speak to the spirits and had not thought of anything. But the hunters were waiting for his answer; he must say something.

"They have said many things," he began, and feeling how his knees were folding under him from fear, he sat down on his haunches. "They have told me that you are to ask me questions."

"Where will we have the most successful hunting?" the old man asked quickly.

"This year the hunters will kill many seal," answered the shaman after a pause. He could tell the answer pleased the old man by the enthusiastic nodding of his head.

"Will we be able to kill another mountain of fat and meat?"

"No, this year you need not even bother looking for it," answered Liok.

"That is true," repeated Niuk, "for never do we catch the whale two years in a row."

The hunters asked questions one by one and the shaman tried to give each one of them a satisfactory answer. It seemed the coming year would not differ greatly from the previous year. But this did not seem strange to anyone—the life of the people of the village was indeed monotonous.

Liok was already beginning to feel relieved that the ordeal might be coming to an end, when suddenly Bei asked him, "Will any of the hunters do combat with a bear?"

Liok desperately did not want to lie to his favorite brother and answered evasively, "You must all take care." But Bei started to ask more specific questions, "Are the 'men of the forest' angry with the hunters? What places in the forest could be the most dangerous?" Then Liok shouted angrily at them, "The spirits have willed to say no more! You must go now!" and quickly walked back into his dugout. "Today I managed to save myself from disaster," he thought to himself, "but someday these lies will be my death."

Soon the sounds of the koldunyii's drums began to reach the ears of the shaman, followed by the sweetish smell of smoke. In the distance he heard the cries and shouts of merrymaking.

The village began to celebrate the festival of Helping the Sun. Holding torches of flaming pine branches, the people lit all the fires at one time. They seemed surrounded by a blazing ring of flames.

Grownups and children alike were jumping in front of the smoky fires. It was believed that smoke cleansed a person of all evil. All those who suffered from aches in the damp weather, whose backs pained them, or who suffered from other ailments, put on all their clothes inside out and stood in front of the billows of smoke, so that it could chase away any evil spirits caught in the folds of their clothing.

Thus the longest night of the year passed quickly for the people. The village was enveloped in a cloud of white smoke. In order to make the fires even smokier, children threw clumps of snow into the flames and branches of wet pine. Everyone forgot their worries and became caught up in the dancing and singing; shrieks of voices imitating birds and beasts traveled from one fire to another. The dugouts stood empty, for even the youngest children did not sleep this night.

Only in one dugout did a fire burn. Beside the hearth sat the figure of a lonely woman. This was Spark. She listened to the noisy festivities but did not share in the feelings of joy. The previous year had been filled with too much grief and she had not yet forgotten Au, nor her son who had been thrown from the cliff by Kremen.

The festivities did not end until sunrise. All day long and the following night the people slept. Then they resumed their usual chores. The women scraped and kneaded the skins they had accumulated during the last year. They made strong thread out of the veins and sewed clothing for the next hunting season. The men mended weapons and made traps and fashioned hooks out of bone for ice fishing. And although the winter held fierce rein over the village, the sun remained in the sky longer and longer each day.

Chapter 25

SOON AFTER THE FESTIVAL of Helping the Sun, the Glavni checked the stores of food. The supplies were very low as was usual for this time of year. But the threat of hunger was not so severe this winter, for by the shore of the sea, buried in ten deep holes, were the meat and fat of the whale that had been killed by the great hunter Au.

Niuk gave orders to prepare for the long journey to retrieve the meat. For two days the hunters repaired their snowshoes. Those whose snowshoes had worn out completely made new ones. The women wove huge sacks of birchwood and tied wide leather straps to them so that they could be carried comfortably on the hunters' backs.

Everyone was faced with many days of exhausting labor. There was so much whale meat buried in the holes that it was impossible to bring it all back at once. And the women could not go with the men all the way to the holes. Nighttime would overtake them and women had to spend the night in their dugouts, so that the female spirits, the mistresses of the forests, swamps, and mountains, who jealously guarded their domains, would not bring harm to them. Niuk decided that they would do as had been done in previous years. The hunters would carry the meat to a place a half-day's journey from the village, then return to the holes again, until in this manner all the meat was moved. The women would then carry the meat the rest of the way to the village before sunset.

On the third day, the hunters set off on the long journey, and Liok went with them. They traveled single file. The snowshoes of the hunters at the end of the line slid easily along the pressed snow, but the going was hard for those in front for they had to make the snowshoe trails in the powdered snow. From time to time the hunter in front would step aside and wait until all the hunters passed him so he could glide along easily behind them.

On the second day of the journey, toward the evening, the hunters saw the column of stones that marked the place where the meat was buried. Old Niuk stepped forward to perform a ritual of gratitude to the whale—the ancestor of their kin, who mercifully keeps his children from starving in the spring. Then they silently pressed forward again, when suddenly a whispered command from Niuk passed down the ranks, "Stop!"

Those in front could see that the snow was marked with footsteps and the stones covering one of the holes were moved, the hole dug up. Shaken with fear and anger the hunters stopped in their tracks. Behind some high rocks they saw the back of a broad-shouldered man wearing tattered clothes. Although they could see only his back, everyone recognized him instantly. It was Kremen. In one hand he held a piece of meat, the other hand was raised above his eyes. He had evidently heard the crunch of the snow under their snowshoes but had confused the direction and was looking the wrong way. Suddenly Kremen turned around.

"Death to Bloody Khoro!" shouted Niuk.

"Kill him, kill him," shouted the hunters and, tripping over each other's snowshoes, they moved toward Kremen.

Kremen tore something from around his neck, raised it in his hand, and shouted, "I am Kremen. I am not Khoro! Liok has deceived you! Kill him, not me."

But it was too late. Before the last words were even out of his mouth, the hunters had knocked him down, and now he was surrounded by them and their spears. When they separated, the mutilated body of the old man lay bloody in the snow.

Suddenly a loud voice rose above the rest. It was Tibu shouting, "He hasn't any teeth. It is not Khoro." It was always said that Bloody Khoro had sharp teeth like those of a shark, and from their touch a person's body became covered with black spots, and then he died.

Old Niuk bent over the body and saw that Tibu was right. "This is not Bloody Khoro," he agreed, "this is a toothless old man." Then Niuk bent down even closer and opened the dead man's clenched fist. A small bone figurine of a man fell out onto the snow. Niuk, who had seen at least three shamans in his lifetime, had seen this figurine many times. It was the fourth, the most important of seven amulets worn by a shaman, and it was supposed always to hang on the shaman's breast. How could this figurine have fallen into Kremen's hands?

"Where is your amulet?" asked Niuk, quickly turning to Liok. Liok paled—for he had lost it in the hunter's sanctuary, when he was bloodying Kremen's clothing.

"Show it to me," ordered Niuk.

Liok's trembling fingers reached beneath his clothes and he found the amulet he had fashioned himself. He breathed a little easier. He took the necklace off and handed it to Niuk.

"This is not it," said Niuk shaking his head. "No shaman has worn one like it. This is the real one. Tell me how it has found its way into Kremen's hands. Tell me why Kremen said that we should kill you."

Liok said nothing.

"I am asking you, shaman," shouted Niuk threateningly.

Liok said nothing.

"Let him ask his spirits," said Bei, coming to his brother's aid. "What mere man can make any sense out of this? Even you, Niuk, do not understand."

"I do not understand," agreed the old man, "but we must understand. Shaman, go ask your spirits!"

Liok looked dazedly at the body that lay in the snow. What could he tell his kinsmen? How could he explain why Bloody Khoro had no teeth! How could he explain how the amulet came to be in Kremen's hands? And why Kremen had shouted out his name?

The hunters, grimly silent, waited for his explanation. In the tense silence Liok could feel his death nearby. As the sun was setting even now, perhaps his life, too, was near its end.

But suddenly he realized that the setting sun could at least postpone his doom. No one could be buried after sunset. "Until the earth has covered the dead one, no spirits can come to me," he said.

Having gained some time, Liok staggered off and fainted in the snow.

When he regained his senses, he was lying behind some rocks, shielded from the wind. When he opened his eyes, the first thing he saw was his brother's anxious face.

"You are alive," said Bei happily. "Your face was the color of the snow itself."

It was completely dark, and seven fires burned brightly in the distance. The hunters had made these to keep the spirit of the unburied Kremen away from them. Until the sun chased away the gloom of night, not one of them would dare venture beyond the circle. "What will I tell them when the sun rises in the morning?" Liok thought desperately, then said, "Bei, my head finds no answer, what shall I do?"

"What can I say?" asked Bei, "I don't understand anything. Who is lying down there on the beach—Kremen or Bloody Khoro?"

"It is Kremen," answered Liok quietly.

"How did he get your amulet?"

"I lost it inside the hunter's sanctuary."

Bei grabbed his brother by the arm. "You have been inside the sanctuary?"

Then Liok told his brother what he had done. As he listened, Bei moved farther and farther away from his brother in horror. It seemed to Liok that Bei wanted to leave him completely, and he quickly said, "Remember what you said when you wanted to save Au from certain death. You told me that I was clever and I would think of something. I did. And now you turn away from me. Would it have been better for Au to die instead of Kremen?"

Bei had no answer for this. He moved closer to Liok, and slowly, barely bringing himself to say the words, said, "Tomorrow they will kill you. They will kill me too and all our brothers because we are the sons of a woman who gave birth to a shaman that deceived his people."

They both remained silent for a long time. When the voices of the hunters inside the ring of fire died down, Liok said, "Let's run away."

Bei thought for a while, and said, "Yes. We will run away. If you are not here, they will never understand what happened. Our brothers will remain alive."

Their snowshoes were beside them, and Bei never parted with his javelin. They tied on their snowshoes, and glancing for a last time in the direction of their kinsmen, went silently into the night.

PART 2

Chapter 1

THE BROTHERS did not run to the east—for there lay the great White Sea. They did not go to the west—for there lived the "forest people," bears of supernatural size, according to legend, who hunted men even as men hunted the other animals of the forest. Nor did they turn their snowshoes north—there it was perpetually night and the spirits of darkness held sway. They went south whence, in the spring, came the swans.

Bei went ahead of his brother. He was the stronger and forged ahead in the powdery snow. The way was difficult, pushing through the thick undergrowth, scrambling over enormous fallen trees, climbing steep hills. At dusk they climbed to the top of a large tree and slept like birds in the thick branches until sunrise. Then they went south again.

The next day they saw a trail; a village was nearby. They could try their luck, or continue onward. Liok was unsure, but Bei remembered stories told by the koldunyii about their nearest neighbors to the south and, as he remembered, he grabbed Liok's arm, urging him to continue past the place. The tales he retold were gruesome indeed, and Liok needed little further urging.

They had eaten nothing for two days, for at the time of their departure there had been no time for provisions. Yet when they came across a small herd of reindeer, and Liok begged his brother to kill one, Bei refused. He knew that at this time of year large wolf packs often shadowed the deer herds, killing off stragglers. A javelin was no protection against a pack of wolves, and Bei turned sharply away from the deer.

Coming up on a frozen swamp where only a few stunted pine trees grew, Bei noticed that the wind whistled sharply along the ground. A dark patch of sky above the forest spread rapidly. Having spent a year among the hunters, Bei knew what was coming—a blizzard! Bei turned back to the forest, searching for cover, but Liok was the first to spot it, a bear's den, only recently abandoned. It would be ample protection from the storm. The brothers had just enough time to gather armfuls of spruce branches which they used to cover the entrance of the lair. Then they lay down on a bed of moss, thoughtfully provided by the previous occupant.

The blizzard descended and the falling snow quickly sealed off the entrance completely. The wind roared through the forest breaking branches off the trees, but the more snow that fell over their hiding place, the less they heard the furious wailings of the storm outside. Sometimes the brothers thought they heard the wailing of human voices, but it was the wind. It grew warmer in the den, and soon the exhausted brothers fell asleep.

Liok awoke, and the storm was still raging outdoors. It was as warm in the lair as in a dugout, but completely dark. Bei did not wake up, so Liok decided that it would be all right to sleep some more. He dreamed of his mother, who was rubbing his head and speaking to him, though try as he might he could not make out what she was saying.

Waking again, frustrated and unhappy, he felt tears on his face.

The brothers did not know how long they were in the bear's den. Perhaps a day, perhaps two. When they finally crawled out, they were astounded by the silence of the sun-drenched white forest. No pecking of a woodpecker, no cry of a raven, not even a rustling in the shaggy spruce trees interrupted the stillness. It was as if the forest were resting after its battle with the storm.

The two fugitives were now weak from hunger, and it was only with great effort that they plodded onward. Just when they thought they could go no further, they came upon a grouse, struggling to free its wings of snow. Bei's arm was swift with the javelin, and there was food to eat.

The following day they crossed another trail, and it was a great curiosity to them, for the snowshoes made in their village were short and wide, but these tracks were long and narrow. Should they go on, or should they follow the tracks to a strange village? Liok suggested that they try their luck here, and Bei agreed. Running like deer through the forest, fearing to meet humans—the thought of more was intolerable.

Following the trail, they soon came across an amazing thing—a large wood grouse with its neck caught in a trap.

"This was done by man," said Bei, leaning over the dead bird. "Our tribe does not know such a cunning thing."

"Let's eat it," said Liok, reaching out to take it. But Bei struck his brother's arm down. "Have you forgotten what happened to the stranger who stole food from our village three winters past?" he said, and pulled Liok away.

Suddenly a man appeared out of the forest thicket. Two grouse hung across his shoulder, one in front and one in back. The man stopped, with his spear held out in front of him. Bei quickly threw his javelin down in the snow and made a few steps toward the man with his arms in the air. Then the man stuck his own spear into the snow and took a few steps toward the brothers.

He was a strong old man, dressed almost exactly like the brothers, except that he carried an ax strapped to his belt. He looked the brothers over curiously from head to toe. Seeing the pieces of whale skin sewn on their clothes, he nodded his head as if to say that he understood from where they came.

Finally he folded his arms across his chest, and Bei, following his example, did the same. Choosing his words carefully, the old man asked them why they had come. It was Bei who related the story that the brothers had agreed to tell. He said that strangers had come from far away and destroyed their village.

The old man seemed to accept this. He nodded his head solemnly and then respectfully touched the necklace of wolves' teeth that hung around Bei's neck. Turning abruptly, he made signs for them to follow, and started down the trail.

As they approached the village, Bei and Liok could not believe their eyes, for streaming out of the village was a pack of snarling wolves—coming straight at them. Bei had already braced his javelin for the onslaught, when the old man shouted something and the "wolves" stopped dead in their tracks. This is great magic, thought Bei, but Liok said, "These are not wolves. See how their tails curl above their bodies." The old man just smiled. "There is much," he thought, "that these young men do not know."

The arrival of two strangers caused a great commotion in the village. The men came running with spears; women and children stared and chattered among themselves.

Bei asked, under his breath, "Shall we tell them you are a shaman?"

"No, please say nothing. The spirits have long ago left me," Liok whispered urgently. "Being shaman was what started our troubles."

Then it seemed that dozens of people were shouting at them at once. Although many of the words sounded familiar, they could not really understand any of it. Suddenly the crowd fell quiet and made way for a tall, broad-shouldered man who walked slowly toward them. The edges of his clothes were trimmed with lynx fur, and Liok guessed that he was the Glavni.

The old man, who was called Kru, began to explain to the Glavni, pointing occasionally at the newcomers and at himself. When Kru had finished his story, the Glavni spoke, and when the Glavni had done speaking, Kru turned to the brothers and said, "Our people do not wish you any harm. They say you should continue on your way."

Liok thought hopelessly about more days of running through the wilderness, and his heart sank. Then Bei said, "Tell the men that they had better kill us. Are we deer, that we should continue to run from hunters?"

The old man translated Bei's answer, and a murmur of approval was heard. Then the crowd backed off, and the men with spears made gestures as if to strike.

"They will kill us like rabbits," whispered Liok.

"Don't be stupid," answered Bei. "Don't you see that they want to test our courage. If we are cowards, they will kill us. If we are brave, I think they will take us in as their own."

The hunters charged at the brothers with fierce cries, lunging and feinting with the spears. The charge ended, and the hunters fell back.

"They will take us into their village," Bei said quietly.

Kru made a sign for them to follow him to a dugout at least three times larger than any they had ever seen before.

The brothers looked around themselves in amazement. The dwellings in their village at home had been dug deep in the ground, with earthen walls. The walls here were made of logs that lay one on top of another, and the floor was at ground level. Each wall had a small opening in it to let the smoke from the hearth out. When the wind began to blow from the north, the old man got up and closed the opening on that side with a plank.

"You don't have this at home," he said, pointing to the opening. "We don't allow the smoke to burn our eyes."

Living in the hut with Kru were the widow of his dead son, her little boy, and the old man's daughter. The women stared curiously at the newcomers and gave each of them a frozen fish. When the brothers had satisfied their hunger, Bei asked the old man how he had come to know the language of the northern people. Kru explained that a long time before, when he was still a young man and was hunting walruses in the sea, the ice on which he had been standing broke away and floated off to sea. He was many days on this floating iceboat until he was picked up by the northern hunters. He had lived with them in their village until the next spring and thus had learned the language.

"But he doesn't speak quite as we do," whispered Liok.

"He must have lived with our neighbors to the south, before they were devoured by Bloody Khoro," answered Bei.

Before long a substantial group of women and children had gathered inside the hut. They looked at the brothers, whispered among themselves, and laughed a great deal. But when three older men entered, one by one, they all fell silent and made room.

Sitting at the hearth, the old men talked something over with Kru.

"They say I should take you as my son," Kru finally said to Bei. "You are strong and will make a good hunter."

"What about my brother?" Bei asked quickly. "He and I are of the same blood."

"We will have enough food for both of you," agreed the old man.

"The time will come when he will be as strong as I am," said Bei. "We both want to be your sons."

Kru translated this for the other men. One of them said something and all of the men burst out laughing. Wiping the tears of laughter from his eyes, Kru said, "In order to be our sons, you and your brother must be born again. We are agreed to that."

"How is that done?" asked Bei of the old man. "How will they do that?" he asked Liok. But Liok did not understand either how a grown man could be born again.

A few days later the brothers understood what had been so funny to the people of the village. On the first night of the full moon, young people gathered brushwood and spruce branches. These they piled up in a large field just outside the village. All the people gathered there, and Kru brought Liok and Bei.

"It looks as if they're going to build a large fire," said Bei. "I don't understand."

Two women appeared, dressed in very large, flowing shirts. Both were shouting and groaning as if in terrible pain, as they climbed atop the pile of branches. Laughing loudly, the people sat down and prepared to watch as Liok and Bei were told to take off their clothes.

"Have the evil spirits robbed them of their senses?" muttered Liok. "Why . . ."

His words remained unsaid, for several old women

toppled them to the ground and quickly took off their clothes for them. Then Kru told them that they must crawl through the wide opening at the neck of the "pregnant" women's shirts, and crawling all the way through, emerge at the bottom, head first, like newborn children.

Liok and Bei did as they were told, amidst gales of laughter, and when they were through, the old women immediately took hold of them and, laying them down on prepared deerskins, wrapped them up very tightly and tied them around with ropes.

"Here we are, born again," shouted Liok to his brother. "Perhaps they want to feed us at the breast now, like infants," he joked.

But that is exactly what happened. The "infants" were carried to a hut in the village where they were left with their "mothers." The people left and the "mothers" commenced feeding their "babes."

"I hope we don't have to remain infants for very long," said Bei, "for we would surely starve to death."

But in the morning Kru came and untied their swaddling. "Now you are our sons," he told them. "When you have learned our language, we will initiate you into the hunters."

Chapter 2

For three days, the newcomers were not allowed outside the boundaries of the village, but they could walk around from hut to hut looking wherever they would.

The village was hidden deep in the forest, some distance from a lake so large that the opposite shore was never visible. The old men of the village told how once, long ago, large boats had come across the lake, no one knew from where. The village, which had stood on the shores of the lake at that time, had been ravaged. It was then that the people moved to the forest, away from the water.

A pack of emaciated dogs wandered among the huts in the village. At first Liok and Bei were afraid each time these strange beasts growled at them. But Kru had thoughtfully provided the brothers with a guide—a young boy who accompanied them everywhere they went. When the boy shouted at the dogs, they fell back growling deep in their throats.

"Why do they want these animals around?" Bei asked his brother.

"Probably to chase away evil spirits," said the younger brother. But after a minute, Liok shouted at Bei, "Why do you ask me? How would I know? I've told you that I am no longer a shaman."

On the third day, their young guide took the brothers to a hut set apart from all the others. When they entered, a man stood up and stepped forward to meet them, signaling at the same time for the boy to go away. In the darkness the brothers could barely distinguish the man's features. Without saying a word he went over to a hole at the side of the room and removed a large pot from it.

Often the people would offer food when Bei and Liok visited their huts. But their host did not feed them. Rather, he reached for a ladle made out of birchwood and, dipping it into the pot, scooped out some darkish liquid. Then reaching his hand inside the pot, he sprinkled some of the liquid on a carved post that stood by the entranceway and muttered something under his breath.

"Look, there is a figurine of a man around his neck," said Liok in amazement.

"And on the wall is a hat like those worn by our shamans," answered Bei. "This must be their shaman."

Their eyes, now used to the dimness, could make out that the old man's hair was plaited into nine braids, and figurines of different animals hung from them. The brothers saw this with some amazement for in their native village, only the High Koldunya wore these.

Liok looked around the hut with great interest. On the east wall hung skins of various animals. The lynx skin was torn in many places, and the fur hung from it in clumps.

"They have the same kind of magic that we do," thought Liok to himself.

The shaman had stopped muttering under his breath. Once again, he dipped his hand into the pot, sprinkled the pole, then brought the pot to his lips and drank from it. When he had done, he handed the pot to Bei. Bei took several gulps and, clicking his tongue in amazement, passed the pot to Liok. The brothers had never tasted anything like this liquid—it was sweet and at the same time burned the mouth. The shaman passed the pot around again, and the brothers drank some more. It tasted better than it had the first time. Their host was generous and, filling the pot again, gave them more to drink. This time the drink was so delicious they did not even feel the burning in the mouth.

The shaman pointed to the pot and then, touching his head, made circular motions around it with his hand. The brothers did not understand why he did this, but thought it very funny and laughed for a long time.

Liok, wanting to show off to his brother that he knew the secrets of the shaman, pointed to the lynx skin on the wall and pretended to throw a spear at it. "If the skin is turned around, you will see a lynx on it," he explained to his brother. "Here, let me show you."

"Wait," said Bei, "my head is spinning. We have been eating all day, and it is spinning as if I haven't eaten for a week."

A woman entered the hut carrying a child in her arms. Clinging to her was another, older child. She sat down in a corner of the hut and began to feed the baby.

Liok was astounded—a woman and children living with a shaman! Suddenly he felt the ground give way beneath him, as if he were in a boat on rough seas. He staggered and fell to the ground. The walls of the hut seemed to come alive, then everything was spinning and he lost consciousness. Within minutes his brother was lying on the floor beside him.

Liok was the first to awaken. He and his brother were lying naked on an elk skin. Their bodies were covered with bright, painted patterns. The shaman, wearing a long robe adorned with figurines and brightly colored stones, danced around them, beating on a drum.

Three old men sat along the wall on their haunches. Liok was afraid. They were surrounded by strange people, with powerful magic that had made them fall asleep. Now he and his brother were naked. In their native village, no one appeared in public without clothes except for execution. Liok leaped to his feet, but nothing happened. The shaman ended his dance and, coming up to the boy, pulled several hairs out of his head. These he threw into the fire.

The three men shouted out a word in unison. One of the voices sounded familiar, and on looking closer, Liok recognized Kru, then he recognized the Glavni. Only the third man was not familiar to him. He was very old, bent with age, and had an enormous beard, which came almost up to his eyes. Then Liok realized that they were performing some kind of ritual over him and his brother.

Kru told Liok that he must leap over the fire in the hearth. It was a large hearth and the flames of the fire were very high. Hesitating only an instant, Liok leaped diagonally across the fire, where the flames were lower. The man with the enormous beard leaned toward Kru and said something to him. Kru smiled approvingly.

"The master says that you have a cunning head," Kru explained to Liok.

The shaman began his mutterings once again and handed Liok new clothes, never worn, made out of deerskin.

"Put them on," ordered Kru. Liok quickly put them on and breathed a sigh of relief.

The shaman took his drum once again and began to dance around the sleeping Bei. He pounded on the drum as loudly as possible, holding it beside the sleeping man's ear and even poking him occasionally, as if by accident, but Bei did not budge. Then, visibly tired from his dancing, he said something angrily to the sitting men.

"Wake your brother," Kru ordered Liok. "The shaman gives you permission to do it."

It took Liok some time to rouse his brother to consciousness. When it came time for Bei to leap over the fire, he unhesitatingly jumped straight across the highest flames and although it was clear that he was burned, he never gave the slightest indication of pain. The old men whispered among themselves once again, and Kru explained, "The elders say that although you are not cunning, you are very brave and will make a good hunter."

Putting on his new clothes, Bei remembered his necklace of wolves' teeth and asked Kru to give them back.

"No," said the old man. "If you want to be one of us, you must not wear anything that comes from other people. Tomorrow you will both go hunting with me and I will teach you everything that is known by our hunters. You must forget everything that has come before in your lives."

Chapter 3

THE FOLLOWING MORNING the brothers slept late. Lifting his head, heavy from drinking the shaman's potion, Liok looked around the hut. Kru was not at home. His daughter, Echo, and the young widow of his dead son sewed small bits of fur on a new dress. Their hands and tongues were completely occupied, for they never stopped talking for a second as their fingers nimbly worked the bone needles.

Noticing that the brothers were awake, the widow stood up and walked out of the hut. The brothers sat and waited for the widow to bring them the pieces of crumbled fish that were eaten for breakfast. Liok fingered the clothes they had been given the day before with admiration. "It is well made," he said to his brother.

"Ours were still good," muttered Bei, "but they took them away from us. They took Au's gift also. He had given it to me so that I would always have the strength of the wolf."

"Kru told us to forget what had happened before in our lives," said Liok. Bei looked at him angrily.

"It will be good for us here," said Liok, trying to pacify his brother. "They have taken us in as their sons."

"Nevertheless, we do not have their blood; we are of a different tribe."

"She is from another tribe too," said Liok pointing at the widow who had entered carrying a birchwood box filled with pieces of frozen fish. "Look how happy she is. She laughs all the time."

At that very instant the woman burst out laughing and, walking past Bei, dropped a piece of frozen fish on his bare knee. In fact she had been named Laughing One, and she was always teasing and making jokes.

Still frowning, Bei was about to pick up the piece of fish, when just then Kru came and told the brothers to get dressed for hunting. Outside the hut, all three tied on their snowshoes and set off on the well-packed trail. Soon they reached a clearing in the forest around which stood a row of huge spruce trees. Kru stopped and so did the brothers. A large carved post, the height of two grown men, stood between two spruce trees. The snow had covered up a good deal of the carving, but they could see that there were seven faces carved one under the other on the pole. There was a small platform made out of flat rocks piled one atop the other in front of the pole, and slightly to the west they could see a row of carved wooden blocks. A row of footprints in the deep snow led to one of the blocks on which the snow had been cleared off. Kru removed his snowshoes, and the brothers did the same.

He took Bei and Liok by the hand and led them to the block. "Here is where my father lies," he said. "This is where all the fathers and grandfathers of our people lie." Then laying his hands on top of the brothers' heads, he made them bow before the block.

"Father who always looks after me," Kru began with emotion in his voice, "accept these two as your grandchildren, even as I accept them as my sons. I will forget my son who died; these two will replace him."

The old man's hands pressed down even harder on their heads and they bent down even more.

"Father, watch over your grandchildren," continued Kru. "They depend on you, and they have no protector stronger than you! Guard their life as you guard mine. Give them weapons and give them fire."

Kru took hold of the brothers' hands and guided them toward the piled-up snow by the block. Liok felt a knife under his fingers and Bei found an ax. Twice more he guided their hands under the snow, and they each found a leather pouch that contained everything necessary to make a fire, and then a knife for Bei and an ax for Liok.

Bei, gloomy since the morning, finally smiled happily. He was very pleased with the bone knife and the ax. No one had such good weapons in their home village. But Liok was even happier, for finally he was a hunter.

The old man embraced the brothers. "Now you have everything that a hunter needs. You will also receive spears and bows and arrows. You will replace my dead son."

The old man led the brothers over to the carved pole. He removed a piece of smoked meat from a pouch at his waist and placing it on the altar in front of the pole he cut it into four pieces. One piece he gave to the spirit of the pole and loudly promised that the brothers would soon bring more good meat if the spirit would aid and protect them during the hunt.

A man named Kibu lived in the village. He was considered the best master of weaponmaking. His work was highly prized by the neighbors to the north and to the south.

Once Kibu had been one of the best hunters in the village, but while hunting one day many years ago, he had been horribly maimed by a wounded bear. He had lain near death for many weeks, and when he finally recovered, his right leg was paralyzed and he could not straighten his back. Only his hands retained their former strength and agility. And Kibu found useful work for them. He learned to make weapons so skillfully out of various stones that there was no equal to him in his village or in the neighboring villages.

Kru now led his new sons to this man's hut. Kibu sat outside by the entranceway. The brothers saw that this was the same heavily bearded man who had been yesterday in the shaman's hut. Before him stood a platform made of one large flat stone which rested on two round ones. The man was bent over it sharpening a slate ax, carefully rubbing it back and forth on a grinding stone.

Kru and his sons stood before him, not saying a word. Kibu did not raise his head. Liok watched his movements with great interest, but Bei was soon bored and he purposely shifted to the side so that his shadow fell across the slab. But this changed nothing. The old master continued to rub the sharp edge of the ax across the grinding stone until he decided that it was sharp enough.

"You have come?" he asked without raising his head.

"We have come," answered Kru. "My sons have nothing to throw."

Kibu raised himself clumsily from the stuffed deerskin which served as a pillow for his twisted body. Dragging his maimed leg behind him, he took several steps back and looked intently at Liok. Finally his face broke into a smile and he said, "He does not need a heavy spear, he needs a light javelin." He spoke in a voice that sounded like a young boy's. He took Liok's hand into his own. Apparently it pleased him a great deal and he began to feel it all over carefully, bending the fingers back and forth.

"This is a good hand for making weapons," he said to Kru; "let me have him as an apprentice."

Kru said nothing. Liok and Bei were supposed to be his

helpers, good strong hunters to make his work easier. He had not taken them out of the forest and made them his sons to now give one up to Kibu, even though he was a good master.

Now Kibu went up to Bei and feeling his chest and arms, said, "This one needs a spear. This one can fight with a bear."

The word for "spear" was the same in both languages and the brothers guessed what the bearded man was saying. Liok felt himself insulted. Although he was not nearly as strong as his brother, he knew that when it came to speed and cleverness he could outshine his brother anytime. Liok looked angrily at Kibu, but the master only smiled back at him and, making a sign with his hand, beckoned Liok to follow him into his hut.

Kibu's dwelling looked nothing like the other huts in the village. The hearth in the center and a pile of sleeping skins were the only indication that someone lived there. All the rest of the space, every corner, was fitted out for the making of arrowheads, spearheads, axes, and other weapons. A flat stone supported by three rocks, similar to the one outside, stood beside the hearth, and beside this was a pile of fine sand. A pot filled with water stood nearby. Within reaching distance lay pieces of flint of various sizes. One wall was completely lined with axes, chisels, and picks of various shapes and sizes. Along another wall were spearheads and arrowheads. In a separate place lay the utensils needed by women in their households—scrapers for cleaning skins, knives, and bone needles.

Kibu proudly pointed to all these things and then to himself to indicate that he alone had made them. He picked up a small ax and an arrowhead and brought them to Liok so that he could look closely at them. As he showed these things, he made sounds with his mouth as if he were eating something especially delicious. The arrowhead was chiseled so carefully and the ax was so smooth and so sharp that Liok was lost in admiration. He remembered the rough, crooked weapons that came from Kremen's hands and looked with new respect at the old master.

In another corner of the hut stood rows of wooden poles for spears. Kibu signaled Liok to take these poles outside. Kru took one of the poles and stuck it in the snow about fifty paces away from the hut.

Bei needed no explanation. He threw the poles one after another with swift sure movements. A group of boys had gathered around them shouting gaily each time a pole sailed past the marked boundary. The pole that had flown the greatest distance Kru himself retrieved and brought inside Kibu's hut. The rest of the poles were gathered by the band of shouting boys.

Now Kibu had to mount a spearhead onto the pole. This was difficult and laborious work. Kibu brought Kru and his sons inside the hut. Motioning for them to sit down, he began his work. First of all, the master placed a pot containing a dark hard substance on the fire. Then pouring some water into a wooden bowl, he coiled a strip of rawhide into it. Then he looked through the assembled spearheads and picked one out. He placed it against one end of the wooden pole and studied it thoughtfully for a while. Then, laying the spearhead down beside him, he began to cut notches in the pole.

By the time Kibu had finished with this part of his work, the dark substance in the pot had turned soft and viscous. The master removed the rawhide strip from the water, squeezed out the moisture, and dried it off a little. Then he dipped the end of the spearhead and the wooden pole into the resinous liquid and, without giving the glue time to harden, he took the gluey end of the spearhead and pressed it and one end of the leather strap into the notch. The free end of the strap was now wound tightly around the juncture of the wood and the spearhead.

Liok could not tear his eyes away from the skillful, sure movements of the master's fingers. Now Kibu was finished and looked his handiwork over with satisfaction. The spearhead seemed to have grown out of the wood. The spear itself might break before the spearhead would come loose.

Bei reached for the spear impatiently, but Kibu moved it away from him and stood it against the wall. The resin needed time to harden. Then the master set to work on Liok's javelin and the whole process was repeated.

When he handed Liok his finished weapon, Kibu said something to Kru, and Kru smilingly translated for Liok, "You have a cunning head. Yesterday you figured out immediately how to jump over the fire without burning yourself. I say that you will outsmart any animal, and he says you can outsmart any rock and will make a good master."

Liok clung to his new weapon, his first one, and shouted anxiously, "No! I am a hunter!"

Kibu laughed, understanding without Kru's help the words of the young man.

Bei too was pleased with his spear. He weighed it in his hand, felt the sharpness of the tip with his fingers, and nodded his head approvingly.

"You know, brother, they make spears better here than they do at home," he said.

Chapter 4

MANY MANY WINTERS had passed since old Kru had fashioned his first trap. He could not count on all the fingers of all the people of the village the birds and animals he had caught in his traps over the years. But now Kru was getting tired. It was getting more and more difficult for him to get around to all the traps hidden in the distant parts of the huge forest. His hands had lost much of their previous skill and strength, and his legs had lost their resistance to fatigue, and when he forced himself to run hard, his chest and throat ached from shortness of breath.

Each time he had prepared to go on his rounds, the old man had sighed for sadness that he had no son to go with him. But this morning the rounds seemed like a holiday to him—for two sons went with him today.

Kru, looking ten years younger, led the way, and Bei and Liok followed him along the trail. Liok looked around happily. Here and there he saw that the snow had been dug up, or he saw a chain of track marks, and in one place a couple of feathers lying in the snow—and he thought nothing of these things as he went by them, for the forest did not speak to him. But Bei and Kru knew instantly what had happened here during the night and in the morning. A hungry fox had come upon a grouse hidden in the snow, but the grouse had taken flight in time, losing only a few feathers, and the fox had gone on his way still hungry.

Suddenly Kru came to a halt and shook his head in distress, angrily pointing to a rabbit's track. Bei did not understand why Kru was angry, but turned to Liok and said, "The rabbit is missing one paw. He is running only on three legs."

Soon they reached an aspen grove. Two sticks stuck out of the ground. They were tightly squeezed together but held nothing more than several short white hairs. "Stupid sticks! They let go their catch," muttered the old man.

"Those hairs are from the three-legged rabbit," said Bei.

Kru dug into the snow around the sticks, and groaning from the effort, dug out a wooden block to which one of the sticks was firmly attached. A knotted leather strap tied the other, shorter stick to it. Kru quickly untied the knot, while the brothers watched his hands carefully. The old man now began to turn the stick in the other direction, and the leather strap was twisted tightly. The old man pulled on it so it would not knot up. He stuck the shorter stick into a groove at the bottom of the longer stick. When he had set the trap, he stuck the point of his spear into it and with a crack the two sticks closed tightly around it.

Amazed at the clever device the brothers laughed happily.

"That's why the rabbit ran on only three legs!" shouted Liok. "His paw got caught, but he was jumping very high and the trap caught only the tip and he was able to get away."

Kru cheered up. He was no longer sorry about the lost rabbit, for he was pleased at how clever his younger son was turning out to be.

The old man told Liok to set the trap. Liok kneeled down

in the snow, and tried to imitate exactly the movements that Kru had made. Kru nodded at him approvingly. At first his clumsy fingers did not obey him and the leather strap would unwind at the wrong time but after several tries he was able to do it smoothly. The old hunter covered the trap with snow so that only the tips of the sticks were showing.

They passed two more traps that were empty, but when they reached the fourth one, Kru smiled with satisfaction for in it lay the dead body of a fox. Kru winked at his sons. The day had not been wasted. He took off his snowshoes and kneeling in the snow began to scoop it away. This trap was not like the other ones. The sticks in this one were longer, thicker, and sharply bent. When the leather strap tightened, the sticks crossed one behind the other and grabbed the animal as if in a hoop. This kind of trap was set for wolves and for lynx.

The trap was better set by two people, for one person would barely have the strength. Straining, the old man pulled the sticks apart and pulled out the fox. Then reaching into his pouch he removed a dried salmon head. Muttering under his breath and bowing down low he threw it over his shoulder. This was an offering to the spirits of the forest to thank them for this rich gift.

The fox was a fiery red color with a snow-white breast. Bei could not tear his eyes away from it. He had killed foxes before, but it had taken much strength and hours of patience and cunning. And here this red-furred beauty had come all by herself to the old man's trap.

Liok had set the first trap and now Kru took strong Bei as his helper. When they had set the trap again, Kru let Bei carry the fox as if he were rewarding him. Bei blushed at the honor the old man was bestowing upon him, and carefully flung the fox over his shoulder.

The hunters went around to thirty traps on that short winter day, and besides the fox, and the rabbit which was finally caught, they also brought home four birds—three grouse and a woodcock. Although they returned to the village late and exhausted, Kru skinned the fox and the rabbit and took the skins along with the grouse to the Glavni's hut. The meat from the fox was thrown to the dogs and the meat from the rabbit and the remaining birds went to Kru's household.

Chattering away and teasing the brothers as usual, Laughing One quickly plucked the birds clean and covering them with a thick layer of clay set them under a mound of hot coals.

The evening was a gay one in Kru's hut. The old man was pleased with his new sons, and the brothers themselves were pleased with the results of the day's hunting. Echo was pleased for she had finished sewing her wedding dress. And Laughing One was laughing as usual. They did not go to sleep for a long time. Kru patiently taught his new sons the language of their new tribe. Only his little grandson, having run around all day, slept peacefully between the warm skins.

Chapter 5

MOST ANIMALS fear man and will not attack him except in desperation. But the old hunters told how they had come across a ferocious bear who even in times of plenty would attack people. This huge bear, his fur a mass of scars, hides in the forest alone. Even at the time of bears' "weddings," when all the bears gather in a clearing in the forest, he stays by himself. For well he knows that given a chance the other bears would rip him to pieces, and he would do the same. A meeting with this hermit bear is a fearful thing.

Even more terrible, however, is the lone wolf. Whether banished by the pack or choosing to wander alone, he roams the forest, an enemy to all living things, until the wolf pack finds him and rips him apart. A wolf like this appeared one day, invading the village in broad daylight. He ran among the huts terrifying the women and children, snatched a three-year-old child in his jaws, and disappeared into the forest. The hunters roamed the forest until nightfall looking for the child in vain. They found only clumps of deerskin from the child's clothing, and a small black stone that the mother had hung around the little boy's neck to protect him from evil spirits.

Five days later the wolf appeared again and carried away a dog. The terrible animal apparently found the village a choice hunting ground. Three days later it burst into the village and carried away a little girl. The people realized that until they had killed the wild beast there would be no safety for them. Mothers were afraid to let their children out to play and they themselves shook with fear when they went for water. Hunters walked around the village day and night with their spears and axes. But on the night of the third day, the wolf attacked one of the guards and ripped his belly open.

The hunter was carried to the burial ground and laid by the altar of the carved pole as a reproach to the spirits for taking such bad care of their children. In the morning when the people came to bury the body they saw that the wolf had chewed it up. Then it was the shaman who said, "Our people have displeased the Spirit of the Forest in some way, and He has sent the wolf to punish us."

Some thought that perhaps the people were being punished for taking in the two strangers. Someone remembered that Bei had worn a long necklace of wolves' teeth around his neck, and soon there was a rumor that the wolves were seeking vengeance. Many had convinced themselves that as long as the brothers lived in this village no one would be safe.

No one said anything to the brothers; they found out about the rumors from Laughing One. She told them everything that was being said, her eyes half-filled with tears. Kru was gone all that day and returned in the evening gloomy and worried. Everyone ate in silence and went to bed immediately after. But no one could fall asleep. From the corner where the women slept, Liok could hear the whisperings of Laughing One and Echo. And the three hunters tossed and turned on their skins until morning.

In the morning, all the people gathered in front of the

Glavni's hut. They were talking back and forth about what was to be done and occasionally glancing at the two brothers standing beside Kru. Then Bei stepped forward.

"People! We have come to live with you because a man is not supposed to live alone like a raven," he began in a loud voice, carefully choosing the yet unfamiliar words. "You have taken us in and you shall not regret it. I will go and kill this wolf, and the children will laugh at it when we hang the head on a post. Let there be no peace for me until I have fulfilled my word."

There was nothing left to talk about. The Glavni nodded his head and returned to his hut. The rest of the people scattered quietly.

It was quiet once again in Kru's hut. The old man had gone quietly and sadly on his rounds without Bei and Liok. For he who has made a promise to his people must think of nothing else until it is fulfilled.

Echo had to go for water, but she was afraid of the wolf. Liok could have gone in her place, but it was not seemly for a hunter to be seen doing woman's work. He took his javelin and went along with her for protection. The little boy went with them as well.

When no one was left in the hut but Bei and Laughing One, she hurriedly pressed something into his hand. It was a charred wolf's tooth.

"I went today and dug in the place where the old men buried your clothes. Perhaps the thing that you brought with you from the place of your birth will help you," she said, then added quietly, "I too keep a small shell from the shores of my native river," and she showed him a tiny, shiny, pearl-colored shell which she had hidden in the moss between the cracks of the walls.

Bei was very happy. This was a tooth from the necklace that had been given to him by Au. A gift was a part of the person who gave it, and now Au, the best of the best hunters, would be with him. Bei felt as if he had suddenly become twice as strong.

"You are the best of the women," he said with embarrassment, "when I kill the wolf, will you take the skin from me?" Laughing One turned red, nodded her head, and ran out of the hut.

Bei, a natural hunter, was able to think like the animals he hunted. When Liok returned from getting water, Bei said to him, "Each time the wolf eats his fill, he does not return until the third day. He was here last night, that means he will not come this night, but tomorrow. In the meantime we must sleep a lot, so that we will have strength."

Bei lay down and fell asleep immediately. Liok tried to sleep, too, but everything kept him awake—the crackle of the wood in the fire, the quiet whispering of the women, and the crunching of snow under the feet of the passersby.

In the evening, Bei, half-awake, and yawning constantly, ate with everyone and immediately went back to sleep.

Bei woke once during the night and saw Laughing One sitting by the fire and slowly adding fuel to it. The night was a very cold one and the frosty air seeping through the cracks in the wood created a cold draft along the floor of the hut.

Next morning, Bei, well slept and cheerful, went with Liok to the burial ground. He guessed that the hungry animal would return to the place where he had left the rest of the uneaten hunter.

He gathered a handful of spruce branches and piled them up by the carved pole and sat down facing the direction from where he thought the wolf would come. He lay down his spear beside him on his right side.

"I will stay here for the night, you go back to the village," said Bei.

Liok reddened from the insult. "You gave your word for both of us. If I am in your way then I will go hunt for the wolf in another place, but I will not hide in a hut while you remain in danger."

Bei gave in at once. He told his brother to sit beside him. It would be better together—if the wolf was not killed with the first blow, then the other could come in and finish him off.

The day passed uneventfully. Night fell. There was a full moon. There was no wind and in the complete stillness of the forest one could easily hear any sound. Everything was going well. They had only to wait.

Some kind of night bird perched on a nearby spruce called out three times, as if to warn them or remind them of something. Bei, his head leaning against the totem pole, made a face each time the bird called out, as if he were afraid that the cries would prevent his hearing other sounds. Then the bird flew away and complete silence reigned in the forest. The brothers still waited.

Finally a dry branch cracked in the distance, then again closer by, and Bei heard the hoarse breathing of a beast. The wolf had come. He came slowly along his previous tracks, scraping his claws against the hard snow crust. Bei silently raised himself up on one knee, firmly clutching his spear in his right hand. The wolf stopped in the same place from where it had jumped the last time. He poised ready to leap. At that very instant Bei flung himself on the wolf. His spear, with the full weight of his body behind it, entered the animal's jaws, and it fell on its side, raising its front legs as if still trying to leap. Almost instantly an ax entered its skull with a crunch, as Liok leaped from behind the carved pole. The wolf was dead. The two brothers stood looking down at him unable to believe their eyes.

They tied three snowshoes together and placing the dead

wolf on them dragged him back to the village. The people gathered at the Glavni's hut once more, but this time with cries of joy and relief. Bei expertly skinned the wolf and the fur hung the full length of a man. Bei held up the skin for the people to see and said loudly, "Fathers, I ask a reward."

"Ask it. What would you have?" answered the Glavni for all of them. A silence fell on the crowd. Bei answered in a loud voice, "I wish to give the wolf skin to Laughing One."

"He is deserving of her," said Kru with a pleased smile on his face. "Yes," said the Glavni. "He has acquitted himself well."

Someone pushed Laughing One forward to meet him although it was unnecessary. She went up to him bravely, and the heavy skin was hers.

Chapter 6

SOON AFTER THAT, Liok also took a wife. He did not choose her. The village elders simply took him to a small hut in which lived a young widow with her twin sons. Every hunter needs a wife, to cook his food, sew and mend his clothes, and keep the fire in the hearth burning. And for a woman it is bad to live alone. She needs someone to look after her and bring food and skins for clothing, especially if she has children.

Liok's wife was called Frightened One. No one ever heard her laugh. Even when she was happy about something, she just smiled shyly. That was how she smiled at Liok when the elders first brought him to her hut. Liok remembered how lonely he had been in his native village, alone in the shaman's dugout. There he had no one to talk with or share his food with in the long winter nights. When Bei had married Laughing One, Liok had felt in the way in Kru's hut. But now he had his own family. The twins soon got used to him. And when he returned from the forest, they ran to meet him demanding that he show them what bird or animal he had caught. Liok quickly grew very fond of the boys.

He was happy living with Frightened One also. Food was always ready for him when he returned from the hunt; his clothes were always dried out and mended. Liok felt as if he was back in his mother's dugout. But his mother had known many interesting stories and legends which she would tell him in the long evenings. Frightened One spoke very little.

When Liok wanted to talk with someone he went to visit his neighbor, Kibu. Although the old master rarely went far from his hut, he knew everything that went on in the village. He knew who had excelled in the hunt and whom Liok could profitably learn from. And although he himself had not hunted for a long time now, he told about the ways of birds and animals in such interesting detail that it seemed as if he had spent his life among them. But his best stories were about stones and rocks, about the wonderful things that skilled hands could make out of a piece of slate or flint. He would show Liok an ugly gray stone and tell him how the outside layers would fall away if he hit it a certain way, and where it would crack if it was hit along the side. Liok watched for long happy hours how the nimble fingers of the old master would turn an ugly stone into an arrowhead or a sharp scraper for skins or into a sharp knife.

One day Liok himself picked up a hammer. His first arrowhead was crooked, but he immediately started to work on another one. The second one was better. Liok was not happy with that one either, and with Kibu's praise and encouragement began a third. It was not long before Liok grew very attached to the old master and very interested in his craft.

The people of the village began to notice that Liok's work was almost as good as the old master's and began to call him Mon-Kibu, which meant young master.

This then was Liok's happy and peaceful new life: in

the mornings he made the round of the traps with Kru and his brother, and the afternoons he spent working under the tutelage of the old master. In the evenings he was surrounded by the happy chatter of his new sons and comforted by the tender smiles of his quiet wife.

Chapter 7

BY NOW THE BROTHERS felt completely at home in their new village. They were able to speak the language, and no one laughed at them anymore when they talked. Both were respected as good hunters. Liok liked the customs of his new people, but he especially liked the fact that he no longer had to pretend to speak with the spirits. He and the old master were good friends and he was very proud of his new name, Mon-Kibu. His hands were becoming more skillful with each passing day and he was more and more pleased with the fruits of his labor.

Spring was near. The snow was melting and soon there were piles of bluish snow only in the deep hollows in the forest. Buds were swelling on the branches, and everywhere the hot rays of the sun fell the earth stirred with living things. Ants scurried back and forth carrying blades of dry grass and tiny twigs in a flurry of spring housebuilding. Flies came alive and their greenish gold bellies glistened in the sunlight. The ice on the lake was covered with pools of melted water and small waves rippled in the narrow inlets of the lake. Flock after flock of migrating birds rested there, and the air was filled with cries of birds from sunrise to sunset.

Liok, like everyone, was glad to see the coming of spring. But along with the happiness came an unexpected longing for his homeland. The earth and the water of the White Sea smelled the same way, the flocks of birds had arrived the same way, and life was filled with the same busy bustle. But at home the coming of springtime was a more momentous event than here, for it meant the end of long hungry days. He wondered which of his kinsmen had not lived to see this spring, and then realized that if they knew the things that he had learned in his new home, they would not have to starve in the winters again. If their weapons were better and if they could make the traps that Kru had taught him, how much easier their life would be.

One day his homesickness grew so strong that Liok no longer wanted to hear the happy shouting of the youngsters in the village and he went for a long hike on the lake. There he came upon a cliff that resembled the Sacred Cliff by the rapids at home. It was at the end of a narrow inlet, and the red, flat granite rose high above the water. As Liok stood looking at it sad and homesick, a swan rose from the ground, flapping its wings loudly as it soared out across the water. He stood and looked after the swan for a long time, remembering the one he had killed that cold night on the Sacred Cliff. He wanted to chisel something onto the cliff as he had done at home. He carried a pick with him in his pouch, and nearby he found a heavy rock to hit it with. So much had happened to him and his brother in the last few months. He wanted to make some record of these events and he began to hammer dot after dot in the red granite. After a while two men on snowshoes appeared on the face of the stone, then a wolf, snarling and angry.

Employed at his favorite pastime, Liok did not notice how the time went. When he finally looked up the sun was setting. He burrowed into the hollow of a nearby tree and when he opened his eyes again the sun was rising over the lake. Although his arms ached from yesterday's work, he began again. He was not at it long, however, when he heard the calls of his son.

"Mother sent me to . . ." started the boy, but when he saw the images on the cliff he broke into screams. Liok vainly tried to quiet the boy—still screaming he ran off into the forest as if all the images he had seen on the cliff were chasing after him.

Now Liok remembered that he had to make the rounds of the traps and set off into the forest himself. Toward mid-day, loaded down with three grouse, Liok returned slowly to the village. His head felt light from hunger, for he had not eaten since the previous morning. Bei came running out to meet him with an angry, worried expression on his face.

"What have you done? Why have you taken up your old ways? The elders have been to the cliff and have seen what you did. Now they are saying that your pictures will lead enemies to the village and it will be pillaged again as it was before. Do you want us to have to run away again?"

Liok stopped in confusion. He had not wanted to bring harm to his new people. How could he rectify his mistake?

"Do not be a coward," he said slowly to his brother, as Bei had once said to him. "Everything will be fine, and the people will be satisfied."

Bei shook his head mistrustfully, but Liok walked bravely toward the gathered crowd. On seeing him, the crowd fell silent. Liok calmly walked into the circle of hunters. Kru spoke first to him, his voice shaking with anger. He reminded Liok how he had found the brothers in the forest and had brought them to his village. How his people had trustingly accepted them as their own. Now how was Mon-Kibu repaying them for all this? By showing their enemies the way to the village by drawing pictures on the cliff?

"Perhaps they have been sent here by our enemies?" someone shouted, and the crowd murmured in agreement.

But Liok raised his hand and said calmly, "Listen to me, my people. The enemies of this village are no different from wolves, and they can be hunted like wolves. We shall make a narrow path leading from the cliff into the forest, away from the village and will build traps at the end of it. Then if enemies try to attack us they will be caught in our traps as we catch animals. And everyone can sleep peacefully at night."

Everyone remained silent in astonishment.

"Hmm. You are a clever young man," said a wizened old man finally. And that evening, everyone kept repeating Liok's words, "Our enemies are like wolves and must be hunted like wolves."

Chapter 8

THE PEOPLE WERE PREPARING for the spring hunt, for the time of the great deer migrations was at hand. Kibu and Liok were loaded down with work. The stores of weapons had to be renewed, and dull arrowheads and spearheads needed to be sharpened, as did the knives and scrapers used to treat the skins. The two were barely able to sleep at all during the short spring nights, and sat all day long bent over their work platforms at their laborious task.

The Glavni of the village had asked for a new flint for his spear, but old Kibu's stores of flint were low. Flint was a rare stone and none was to be found anywhere in the vicinity of the village.

Kibu removed his carefully guarded last piece of flint and, thinking for a minute, handed it to Liok. He said nothing, but the young man understood very well how important his task was.

Liok wrapped the piece of flint in some wet leather and left it there overnight. In the morning he began to work on it. Liok studied the stone for a long time, guessing which way the layers and veins ran. Then with sharp accurate blows he removed layer after layer of superfluous material from the rock until it was the shape he needed. Kibu looked over his shoulder and nodded his head approvingly. Now came the hard part—to work the rough shape into a finished spearhead. Liok sat at this task for a long time. Tiny, thin pieces, resembling fish scales, were chipped away from the rock by his skillful hands. The rock, now rounded in the middle, became sharper and sharper around the edges and toward the point, until it resembled a leaf fallen from a tree, with a notch at one end for the spear itself.

Kibu took the finished spearhead in his hands and, looking it over from all sides, said that it had been a long time since he had seen such fine work. But Liok was still unsatisfied. It seemed to him that there was an unnecessary bump on one side, and he wanted to smooth it out. He gave it one last tap and the spearhead broke in two. All that work gone to waste! And the worst part was that there was not another piece of flint to be had in the entire village.

Kibu did not even attempt to console Liok, for he well knew what a tragedy this was for a master.

As soon as Liok returned to his hut, Frightened One saw that something bad had happened. He never even touched his food. When the twins ran in shouting and laughing, their mother pushed them out and came to sit by Liok's side to find out what had happened. But Liok remained silent.

Finally, he said, "They say that the village you come from is rich in flint beds. Do you know where to find them?"

"When a woman becomes the wife of a hunter from another village, she must forget all the secrets of her home," answered Frightened One in a quiet voice. "I do not know where to get flint."

"You are a bad wife," said Liok. "Laughing One would tell Bei if he needed to know."

"No! I am a good wife," shouted Frightened One. "I will show you what you want."

Liok wanted to take his brother along and sent Frightened One for him, telling her to say nothing to Kru or Laughing One. But Bei and Kru had taken a boat downstream to go fishing and would not return for three days.

"So we will go alone," sighed Liok. They decided to leave at dawn, Liok carrying with him a bag of deerskin tied to his waist, and an ax. His wife took along food for the trip.

Quietly stealing through the village, they came to the bank of the river. Then they traveled slowly along the curves in the riverbank. Liok was impatient with every delay, for he wanted to be back home before sunset. He imagined how he would lay out the precious pieces of flint before an astonished Kibu. And he, Liok, would make many spearheads, even better than the one he had broken. He would work without stopping to make as many as possible—for the days of the deer hunt were close at hand.

Frightened One seemed pleased with every delay, for with every step forward, she grew more frightened. What would happen if her former kinsmen caught sight of her on their native shores? She knew that when a girl had left her village, she left it forever, and she was never for any reason to return to it. She had only dared to go against this taboo for her husband's sake. And now as she walked along behind him she recited every oath she knew to try to avert the disaster she knew she was courting.

Liok stopped to wait for his frightened wife to catch up. Sensing her anxiety, he took her hand and asked tenderly, "Are you afraid?"

"Yes, I am afraid," she said, "Oh, how afraid I am!"

"Don't worry, I will not let any harm come to you."

"I am afraid for you too. What will the elders say?"

Only then did it occur to Liok that he should have asked the Glavni's permission.

"Shall we go back?" asked Frightened One hopefully.

"But the village needs flint," said Liok as much to himself as to his wife. "Let's go on," he said firmly and started walking ahead.

"In my heart I see grief," said Frightened One quietly and went after him.

"Your heart always sees nothing but grief," said Liok over his shoulder.

Frightened One remained silent the rest of the way. They walked for a long time, and only when the sun showed that it was past midday did she touch Liok's shoulder and say, "Here."

Liok stopped. Straight ahead of them, on the other shore, was a bank of dark cliffs while in the middle of the river were two shoals of flint, one closer to the shore they stood on, and the other closer to the other shore.

Liok estimated the distance to the closest shoal and then picking up a long stick which lay nearby, he stuck it into the water and leaped across. "Here," he shouted to Frightened One, "follow me."

"I dare not leave the shores of my husband's land," she said. "Why do you shout? You can be heard in the village."

Liok found no loose rocks on this shoal and jumped over to the one closer to the other riverbank. Some low bushes grew there, and beneath one of them Liok noticed two sticks sticking out of the ground. Liok went up to them and placed his stick between them. They instantly snapped shut around it. Then he saw a piece of flint on the ground, and digging around in the sand found many more. "These will make excellent spearheads," he thought happily. Very soon his bag was almost full.

It was harder now to get back to the first island because of the heavy bag he carried; and harder still to jump back onto the bank where his wife waited nervously. When he reached her, he handed her the full bag and said, "Let me have your bag. I am going over to the other bank where there are many more larger pieces of flint."

His wife stepped back from him in horror. "No one from our tribe is allowed to set foot on that shore," she said with a firmness which astonished Liok. "There will be war! There will be many deaths!"

Liok saw that she was right. He had gathered enough flint anyway. Flinging the heavy bag over his shoulder, he made his way back to the village with his wife. As they got closer to home, anxious doubts began to assail him. Had he been wrong to go against the customs of his people? But when he thought of the riches on his back he felt better. The flint was so needed by the village, and Kibu would be pleased.

But Kibu was not pleased. When Liok poured the contents of his leather bag out before the old master and began to count out how many spear and arrowheads they would be able to make, Kibu realized immediately how his young assistant had spent the day and where the flint had come from.

"Arrows and spears made of this flint will bring our people not luck, but disaster!" he said severely. "Put it all back in the bag and we will go to the Glavni."

The Glavni ordered that the elders be called together immediately. As the old men entered the Glavni's hut one by one, Liok could tell by their anxious frowning faces that they already knew about the new misfortune that their adopted son had brought upon the village.

"It is clear that our neighbors will make war on us," said the Glavni, "for they will not tolerate one of our men on their soil."

"But I never went on their shore!" exclaimed Liok. "I gathered the flint on the island in the river."

The old men were visibly relieved, and began to discuss among themselves what steps to take next. Liok was also relieved that his transgression was not so serious, and he began thinking of all the weapons he would make to atone for his sins.

But Kru stood up and said, "We must throw what does not belong to us into the river as quickly as possible." And all the elders agreed with him. They all rose and left the Glavni's hut. It was clear that no one wanted to touch the bag lying in the center of the hut, and the Glavni ordered the astonished Liok to carry it to the river. Liok had expected anything but this. Angry and humiliated, he walked to the river, followed by all the people of the village. When they reached the water, the Glavni ordered Liok to throw the bag in. It made a loud splash in the water and sank to the bottom.

"Go to your hut," ordered the Glavni, "and stay there until we decide what to do with you."

Liok was happy to leave as quickly as possible to escape the eyes of the villagers. But he found no comfort in his hut. There was no fire in his hearth and Frightened One sat hunched up in a corner. When she raised her face to Liok's he saw that it was bruised and bloody. The women had beaten her for bringing the danger of war to the village and for breaking the rules of the elders.

Liok sat down beside her. Frightened One pressed herself close to him like a child. Mosquitoes began to fill the fireless hut and their monotonous whine seemed to fill the air with more sadness.

The twins returned late to the hut, for it was warm and children gathered their own food all day. Seeing that their mother had no interest in them, they curled up inside the skins like two little animals and went to sleep.

Liok and Frightened One sat huddled together for a long time in the unheated hut, trying to guess what the elders would decide. Then they too fell into a light sleep.

Early in the morning the old master woke them. "Get up Mon-Kibu, there is much work to do. Soon the deer herds will come. Your hands have saved your head, this time."

Frightened One set to making a fire and soon the clouds of smoke forced out the flies and mosquitoes. The hut was once again filled with warmth and life and it seemed to Liok and Frightened One that danger had passed them by.

Chapter 9

WHEN THE SUN SHINES hot all day, it is not good to sit in the dark huts. A dampness rises from the earthen floor and seeps through all the skins, and even the dried meat hanging from the ceiling gets covered with mildew. The air in the unheated huts becomes dank and musty. And each spring Kibu's old joints ached, and all his bones felt mashed. If he sat inside his hut for even a little while, a hacking cough began to rack his body and his hands began to shake so that his hammer blows were not true. So with the coming of spring, the old master brought all his work platforms outside and sat in the sunshine.

So it was that morning, a warm and sunny one, when Liok and Kibu sat at their labors. Kibu was sharpening an ax, and Liok was finishing a scraper to be used for cleaning skins. He had made it from the broken arrowhead, and turned it into a very clever device. For while it was a scraper on one side, the other side was as sharp as a knife and could be used for cutting skins. Both edges were sharpened and he had only to attach it to a wooden handle. Liok was just reaching for the piece of wood, when he heard cries at the other end of the village, "Gadflies! The Gadflies have come."

Hearing the cries of the boys, the hunters came pouring out of their huts, as did the Glavni. After the long wait, the time had finally come to prepare for the deer hunt. The Glavni calmly gave orders to the hunters. Hunters and boys were sent out to the forest to wait along the side of the river where the migrating deer would come.

Only Liok remained at his place. There was much work for the masters and he did not expect old Kibu to release him for the hunt. Liok sighed and his hammer beat out faster on the stone platform.

A noisy group of hunters passed them, and Bei left the group to speak to Liok. "Are you coming?" he asked. "Are you an old man to deny yourself the pleasures of the hunt?"

Liok said nothing but glanced at the old master, who was slowly rubbing the edge of an ax against the polishing stone.

"Let my brother go," said Bei to Kibu. "You were young once. How can he sit here, when everyone else is going?"

Kibu raised his head and looked at Liok's sad face, then he looked at Bei. After a long moment he said, "Go ahead. I will finish up myself."

The hunters arranged themselves in a long chain along the riverbank. Picking a tree, each one climbed up into it and camouflaged himself with leaves and branches. Then the waiting began.

Waiting was especially difficult for Bei, for he had never known this kind of hunting before. At home, they hunted deer in twos and threes and sometimes all alone. Success depended on the speed and endurance of their legs, and on the sureness of a hunter's eye and throwing arm. Here everything was different. They had to sit hidden in a tree and patiently wait for the herd to pass. Bei was bored and angry.

"Our hunters would never hide, wasting time while they waited for a herd that might never appear," he whispered angrily to his brother.

"The elders say that if the herd is chased into the deep part of the river, we will be able to kill many deer and we will have much meat."

But in a while, other hunters began to lose their patience too. What if the herd had chosen another place to cross the river, while they sat in the trees like owls.

Soon, however, they heard in the distance the crackling of dry underbrush. Woe to the hunters if even one deer sensed the presence of men. They would disappear into the forest instantly and that would be the end of the hunt. The sound of many hoofs came closer. Then a buck, the leader of the herd, emerged from the forest. He walked calmly, followed by the obedient does and fauns. Bei had never seen so many deer together at one time. When the herd had passed the line of hunters in the trees, one of the boys slipped out and ran back to the village with the happy news. The others, too, left their perches and silently followed the herd. The deer approached the river oblivious to their danger.

The herd entered the cold water of the river slowly, going in deeper and deeper, and finally began to swim across the current. When the first deer reached the middle of the river, women and children jumped out from the bushes on the other side, and began screaming and shouting. The frightened animals tried to turn back, but there were people raising a ruckus on the other bank as well. The deer all crowded together in one group, and began to swim with the current. The villagers ran along both shores not letting the animals leave the water. The hunters, in light boats, began their killing.

The fast current of the river carried the herd while the

hunters killed them with their axes and their spears. The water turned red with blood, and over half the herd died, before any were able to get away. And although many of the dead deer floated away on the swift river, the people dragged in many more of them, and the day's catch was enormous.

Chapter 10

FIVE FIRES in the clearing of the village sent bluish wisps of smoke into the sky in celebration of the successful hunt. The shaman had already performed the ritual of peace-making with the souls of the dead animals, and the young hunters had performed the dance of the reindeer. The feasting was in full progress. The people's hands and mouths glistened with fat. Even the ever-hungry dogs were so full that they no longer fought over bones. The salty blood made everyone very thirsty, but the hunters were too exhausted to go for water. Two women finally dragged themselves up and, carrying large pots, went to the river. But soon they came running back. Out of breath and their hair loosened in the sign of disaster, they stopped before the Glavni. The happy noise of the feasting died. Everyone looked at the women to hear what they would say.

"There is a boat on the river," said one of the women, still panting for breath.

"There are men dressed in red and they carry red arrows," added the other.

The men leaped up from their places, and the mothers loudly called their children together. The hunters quickly gathered their spears. The Glavni rose to his feet giving a sign to the elders and went to the river. Only Kru and Kibu remained behind. They quietly called Liok to their side. "Now neither your head nor your hands can save you. Go into the forest for three days and three nights."

Liok did not understand what was happening, but obediently went around the village into the forest. When the young man had disappeared from sight, Kru and Kibu hurried after the Glavni and the elders.

Before going out to the river, the Glavni stopped in his hut and took three arrows with him. He kept one and handed the other two to Kru and Kibu. The three men straightened their clothes and, carrying the arrows pointed toward the ground, descended to the riverbank.

A large boat floated in the river. Two oarsmen held it steady with their oars. Between them stood an old man wearing clothes painted in bright red ocher. In his outstretched hand he held a bloodied arrow pointed toward the village. This was a declaration of war.

The Glavni, Kru, and Kibu walked up to the water and stretched out their arrows, with the points to the ground, a sign of peace.

The boat came closer and the man in red took the outstretched arrows. The acceptance of the gift meant that they were willing to settle their differences peacefully.

"A man from your village has broken the agreement of our grandfathers and has taken what belongs to us," said the man in red.

"The man from our village never set foot on your shore," answered the Glavni calmly.

"But he took that which belongs to us."

"On the bottom of the river you will find that which belongs to you," and the Glavni pointed to the place where they had thrown the bag containing the flint.

When the bag had been retrieved and the contents spilled on the bottom of the boat, the man in red once more pointed the arrow at the village. The dispute was not yet settled.

"You say that the man from your village has not broken the agreement. But there were other footsteps beside his. Smaller ones belonging to a woman. The man was led there by a daughter of our tribe. Give her to us, we will punish her." The bloody arrow dropped slightly.

The old men did not answer, and the arrow started to rise once again. The Glavni looked at Kru and Kibu, who sadly lowered their heads. Then he said, "It will be as you say." And turning to the people behind him said, "Bring the woman and her children."

The twins were nearby on the shore and they were lifted into the boat. Not understanding what was happening, the boys laughed happily at the thought of going for a ride.

Soon they also dragged the sobbing woman to the boat and tied her hands and feet. Then the man in red handed the bloody arrow to the Glavni, in a sign that the talks had ended peacefully. The boat slowly pushed away from the shore and traveled up the river. No one moved until the boat disappeared behind a bend in the river and they could no longer hear the cries of Liok's wife. Thus the village was saved from the threat of war with its neighbors.

Liok returned to the village that same night, although he had been told to stay away for three days. But when he quietly entered his hut, he found it cold and damp. Stretching out his hands in the darkness he felt his way to the sleeping skins, but neither his wife nor his children were at home.

He knew then that some terrible harm had come to Frightened One, for a woman was supposed to sleep only at her hearth. If she was not there, then she was nowhere in the village. Had she been taken away by the stranger in the boat? If a woman was returned to her native village then she was sentenced to die. And the sins of the parents fell also on their children; that meant that the twins . . .

Liok ran to Kibu's hut. Old people do not sleep much and their sleep is very light. Kibu said, "In the morning go to the Glavni. He will tell you everything." Liok asked one question after another but all in vain. Kibu said not another word.

Neither man could sleep, and soon Kibu got up and went outside to the polishing stone.

The night seemed endless to Liok as he waited for the sunrise. Finally he could wait no longer and went to Kru's hut. Everyone was asleep there.

"Where is Frightened One?" shouted Liok.

"Go to the Glavni. He will tell you everything," said Kru, echoing the words of the old master.

"You tell me!" screamed Liok, forgetting himself in his fury.

"Frightened One was given back to her tribe," answered Kru slowly. "She has broken the traditions of her fathers. She will be buried alive."

"But I am the guilty one. I am the one who should be punished," shouted the youth.

"They cannot punish you, you are from our tribe. They had prepared to go to war, but did not want to spill the blood of many. We gave them the one of theirs who went against the order."

"And her children?" whispered Liok in horror. Laughing One moved in her sleeping bag and sighed softly, but neither she nor the old man answered him.

Liok stood leaning against the wall until he heard the laughing voices of the young women going for water. Kru woke Echo. Stretching and yawning sleepily, she hurried to join her friends on the way to the river. The day in the village began as usual.

Liok's knees shook under him when he left Kru's hut to go to the Glavni.

"It was I who broke the tradition," he said in a barely audible voice. "Frightened One was innocent. She could not disobey me. I will go to them. Let them punish me instead."

"How can you go if we do not let you?" asked the Glavni in surprise. "Is it possible that in your village everyone did as he pleased?" Then he softened his voice and said, "She is no longer among the living. But we need you. You are a good master. In the fall we will send you with the other unmarried hunters to pick a wife."

Blinded with tears he was not supposed to shed, Liok went back to his hut. He stood outside for a few minutes not wanting to enter the deserted dwelling. Then someone took him by the hand and led him away. It was old Kibu.

"It will be better for you here," he said leading Liok to his own hut.

Chapter 11

THE LIFE IN THE VILLAGE, so recently threatened by bloody conflict, continued as before. No one blamed Liok, although his willful actions had brought the people to the brink of destruction. Everyone understood that he had not meant any harm. The younger hunters often talked to him about how they would all go in the fall to choose brides from the neighboring villages. Liok said nothing—he could not forget Frightened One, and it was bitter for him to think that everyone in the village had forgotten her so quickly. This, however, was not true. The women, when they were not with their men or with their children, talked often about her, and they took turns carrying food each night to Frightened One's hut to feed the spirits of the dead woman and her children.

Liok moved in completely with Kibu. They cooked their food together and slept together. But now the tapping of two hammers was rarely heard by the old master's hut, for Liok sickened of his once-beloved work. And he left the village as often as possible to go hunting with Bei. Old Kibu shook his head reproachfully but said nothing.

Several small islands could be seen in the distance from

the shore of the lake. In the winter the hunters reached these islands by crossing the frozen water, to hunt for lynx, but no one came here in the summer. The forests and the river, rich with game and fish, supplied plenty of food for the villagers and they had little need to brave the dangers of the lake. But the brothers liked to hunt there because the lake reminded them of the sea at home. On these islands they were alone and could speak in their native tongue. They went often in a small light boat made from a hollowed-out tree trunk.

It was getting on toward autumn, the best time for fishing in the lake. The brothers lit a torch and attached it to the prow of their boat. The light from this flame lit up a portion of water beneath the boat and while Liok paddled the boat slowly across the lake, Bei leaned over the side, harpoon in hand, and watched the illuminated bottom of the lake pass by. He could see clearly the dark blue backs of the passing fish—sometimes large-headed eels, and sometimes long-headed pike. Bei never missed, and the fish came floating to the surface belly up. The boat gradually filled with an excellent catch, but Bei grumbled nevertheless.

"Here we are, floating like logs on the water. What kind of hunting is this? On the sea man can test his strength and courage. But here . . . if you get something—good, if you don't—that's all right too! Even in the forest, we don't hunt, but hide like moles."

"Yes, but if the Spirit of the Sea doesn't send game," reasoned Liok, "the entire village starves.."

"If we taught our people how to set traps in the forest, they would not starve in the spring," said Bei thoughtfully. "I know how to make traps for every kind of animal now."

"And I have learned how to turn black stones into good weapons," said Liok. They were silent for a while. Then Bei looked at his brother and said, "What if we . . .?"

"I think about that all the time. I eat something and think, 'How are our people? Have they had good hunting this summer?' "

"But what could we say about why we ran off? Why did we come back? How could we explain why Kremen had the figurine from your necklace?"

Liok shook his head. "I don't know."

Evening came and the fishermen made a fire on one of the islands and hung the fish to smoke above it. Then they lay down beside the fire. As he was falling asleep, Bei said to his brother, as he had said once before, "You are clever, you will think of something."

Toward morning Liok woke Bei up. "You sleep too long. I have already thought of something and you keep on sleeping and sleeping."

Bei woke up instantly. "Tell me quickly," he said to his brother.

"This is what we must tell our people. When the hunters came upon Bloody Khoro in the sanctuary, he was afraid to show himself and released Kremen, in whose body he had been living. So the man by the whale pits was the real Kremen, who had not dared to return to the village lest everyone think he was still possessed by Khoro. So he fed himself on the whale meat in the pits."

Bei listened carefully and nodded his head approvingly. Then he asked, "What about the figurine? How did Kremen get ahold of it?"

"The figurine? We can say that a forest spirit ripped it off my neck and gave it to Khoro. That is why Kremen had it. And you and I left for the south because my spirits willed us to. They told us that we would learn to make traps and better weapons, so that our people would never again starve in the spring. We learned how to make these and returned to our native soil."

Bei looked at his brother with admiration. Perhaps it would work. . . . Wouldn't old Niuk be amazed when he saw how two sticks could catch a grouse? And Bei laughed aloud imagining the surprise of their kinsmen at the wonders they would show. "Let's leave today!" he said and began hurriedly to remove the smoked fish from their perches.

"This means, though, that you will be a shaman again," said Bei after a few moments thought.

"Oh no! No! No! No!" shouted Liok. "I want to be like the others. I will say that the spirits have punished me for losing their gift, and they have gone from me forever. I want to be like everyone else. I never was a real shaman and I never saw any spirits anyway."

"What do you mean you never saw any spirits? You always said, 'My spirits said this and my spirits said that.' Do you mean you were lying to us?"

"I did not want to . . . but it happened almost by itself. . . . Don't you remember how Kremen ordered me to find food for the village? It all began with that swan."

But Bei still could not believe what his brother was telling him. "How can you say that you never saw the spirits? Why even the hunters saw Roko! He showed himself to us on the night of the initiation rites."

Liok laughed quietly, remembering how he had shaken his fist at the hunters and how they had backed off from him. "That was not Roko. It was I."

Bei, speechless with surprise and anger, could not utter a word. He turned on his heels and ran into the forest.

Liok found his brother lying on the ground, his face pressed into the soft moss. Liok tapped him lightly on the shoulder.

"Go away!" shouted Bei. "How can I return to my kinsmen with such a liar?"

Liok sat down beside his brother and waited patiently until he had calmed down. Then he told him how Fox Paw had tried to destroy him, how Kremen had threatened to throw him into the rapids, how Au had been unhappy because Kremen had given him a crooked harpoon and he, Liok, had helped him by giving him the harpoon that had belonged to the last shaman. . . .

The brothers talked for a long time on the deserted island and did not return to the village until evening.

Bei wanted Laughing One to go away with him and was very pleased to find her alone in the hut when he returned from the fishing expedition. He sat down by the hearth and told her what he and his brother planned to do.

"Will you go with us?" he asked.

"I cannot speak your language," she answered. "Your women will not accept me."

"You will learn quickly," Bei said to her. "We did not know your language either."

"But my sister is here and all my friends," said Laughing One, "and there everyone will be a stranger. How will they treat me?"

Bei himself was worried about this, but continued to coax her anyway. "But you will be with us . . ."

Laughing One did not know what to do. She was afraid to go with them but did not want to part with Bei either.

"Yesterday my son left with the other children to hunt ducks," she finally answered. "When he returns I will give you my answer."

"Very well. I will wait," agreed Bei.

The next morning when the brothers went to look at the traps Bei said to Liok, "We must not leave yet. It is very cold in the forest. We must wait until there are mushrooms and berries. Now we will have nothing to eat along the way. And Laughing One is waiting for her son to return from hunting ducks."

Liok said nothing. He understood why Bei now wanted to postpone their plans.

Chapter 12

ONE MORNING Liok got up, broke his fast with Kibu, and, as he always did of late, prepared to go hunting. He was halfway out the door when the old master stopped him. "Are you no longer to be called Mon-Kibu?" he said. "If you are not careful the stones will no longer obey you. Summer is almost upon us, and the time of trading is soon. Young hunters from other villages will come to choose brides, and the old hunters will come to trade weapons. What will our tribe have to show? I am old. Come, Mon-Kibu, sit beside me and let us work together."

Liok hesitated for only a moment, then sat down at the work platform. Soon the sound of double hammer blows filled the air around the old master's hut.

Liok's work did not go well at first. He rushed as though he wanted to make up for lost time. The stones slipped from between his fingers, and the hammer did not strike where he aimed it. Liok glanced at the master, but Kibu sat hunched over his own work and paid him no mind. Then the young man settled down and the slivers of stone fell away evenly as he regained his former skill. Liok was happy beside the old master as he had been before.

Several days were passed like this. Liok was sharpening a flint when the Glavni entered the hut. He looked approvingly at the finished weapons, but asked the old master, "Will we have enough?"

Without a word Kibu lifted up a cover of skins and revealed a second pile of newly finished weapons, all beautifully made of flint.

"You have worked hard," said the Glavni. "You have not wasted time."

"Yes. We've had quite a bit of work, Mon-Kibu and I," said the old man, trying hard not to show how pleased he was with the Glavni's praise.

During these days the women of the village knew no rest. The young girls of marrying age were preparing their bridal costumes, and all was confusion. Mothers would visit one another hoping only to sneak a look at the costume of the other's daughter, then hurrying home a mother would start from scratch redecorating her own daughter's bridal dress. The more beautiful a bride's costume, the more the hunters from the neighboring villages would look at her.

Although Echo had no mother, she prepared herself as well as all the others. Old Kru had provided his daughter with many fine skins, and Bei and Liok had not forgotten their adopted sister either. Laughing One helped with the sewing.

Finally the maidens' preparations were complete. One day toward evening the maids, all dressed in their bridal finery, came out of their huts. Singing special ritual songs, they circled the village three times, a sign for the hunters to go out with bids of welcome for the men of the neighboring villages.

The guests arrived on the following day and entered the village with great ceremony. Leading them was the Glavni of their tribes. He carried a large, beautifully embroidered bag filled with wares for trade. After him came the older hunters, and last of all came the long-awaited bridegrooms, carrying gifts of furs and jewelry.

The guests were invited to seat themselves in the clearing in the center of the village. The old men stooped down on their haunches and carefully spread out their wares before them. To their left sat the grooms, silent and grand, like the figures on a totem pole. Each held his gift bundle in his lap.

The grooms waited impassively, even shyly, but the old hunters were wasting no time. The trading began in earnest almost immediately, and the Glavni, along with Kru and Kibu, was examining the weapons for trade. All were made of inferior yellow flint, though the Glavni had noticed that one of the older men had a bag tied to his waist that was filled with something heavy. Better wares were being held in reserve.

"Do you see?" said the Glavni quietly, pointing at the bag.

"I see," said Kru, though he was looking not at the bag but at the bridegrooms; in fact, he was looking at one of the young men in particular.

"Your eyes have probably spied a suitable husband for your daughter by now," said the Glavni, "so would you kindly turn them to these weapons? The bargaining is about to begin."

Kru stepped over to the weapons. He picked several up and turned them over. After looking carefully, he said, "We will not take these." While the visitors took back the rejected specimens, Kru continued his examinations and Liok, at a sign from Kibu, brought out their own weapons and laid them out opposite the others.

The eyes of the guests gleamed, though no one moved even a muscle. Kibu demanded more for a trade, and the guests whispered among themselves. Then ten red flint spearheads appeared from the bag.

And so the bargaining went, for a long time until both sides had agreed that the exchange was fair. Then the Glavni ordered that refreshments be brought, and the trading was done.

The women quickly set dishes of fish, bird, and deer meat, berries and roots before the guests. The young men brought three large pots of "happy water" and set the largest before the oldest men, another before the older hunters, and the last before the bridegrooms. Everyone ate and drank with gusto. Everyone but the bridegrooms, that is, who sat as if rooted to the ground—for they were to have neither food nor drink until they had chosen their brides, a business that, with the eating done, was close at hand.

The maidens approached, led by the old women of the village, and sat down in a row, opposite the grooms. Each was beautifully arrayed in her bridal costume, and the choices were not easy. The young men looked carefully at the brides, trying to see which was prettier, trying to guess which would be the best worker. Gathering some courage, the girls too raised their eyes and began to study the young men.

Echo, looking beautiful in her finery, had noticed from under her lowered lashes that two young men were staring at her. Both had wide shoulders, strong necks, big strong hands, and both looked to be good hunters. But when Echo looked closely at them, she noticed that one of them looked a little like Bei—he had the same wide, kind face. Echo had just had time to notice that when Laughing One came up to her and quietly whispered in her ear, "Pick the one on the end. You will be as happy with him as I am with Bei." She meant the one whom Echo was looking at. His neighbor continued to stare at her for a while longer but, realizing that she favored another, sighed quietly and began looking the other girls over. This year the young men had many girls to choose from—there were nine prospective bridegrooms and thirteen available girls.

When the old women decided that the young people had had enough time to look each other over, they made a sign for the young men to get up. Some of them shuffled their feet in one place, unsure of their choice, or perhaps unsure their suit would be accepted.

But the young hunter who resembled Bei did not hesitate. He stepped forward and handed his gift to Echo. Echo accepted it with trembling hands and stood with her eyes lowered. The young man unrolled the luxurious lynx skin and took out the necklace that had been wrapped in it. Echo smiled happily—no one, it seemed to her, had ever had a necklace as beautiful as this one. Green, yellow, and white feathers stuck out in all directions. Woven into it were bits of squirrel tail and in the center was the skull of an enormous pike, surrounded by beaver teeth. Hanging from separate leather straps were some wolves' teeth and a bear's claw. Echo had chosen well—the young hunter had already killed a bear, a wolf, and a lynx.

The young man, proud that his gift was so well liked, hung the necklace around Echo's neck. She took her husband-to-be by the arm and led him to her father's hut. Her relatives followed—a pleased Kru, Laughing One and Bei and their son, and a sadly smiling Liok.

The guests remained in the village for three days. It was a time of festivities. The old men feasted and drank in the shade of the trees. The young hunters held competitions and measured each other's skill and strength—they threw spears, shot arrows, and wrestled with each other. The bridegrooms tried especially hard to acquit themselves well before their future wives.

The older men watched and recalled the days when they were young and had participated in the games. In the evening huge fires were made and the hunters danced and sang.

Finally the time for departure came. The air was filled with wailing songs as the mothers lamented the departure of their daughters. They would never see them again. The four unchosen maidens, who had cried through the three days of festivities, were now relieved that they did not have to leave their native village. The brides feared the prospect of a new life in a strange village, even as they joyfully anticipated having their own huts and the reunion with older sisters and aunts who had left for this new home many years ago.

When the sun rose above the forest, everyone went to the shores of the lake. The guests did not even glance at the boats that floated readily on the shores of the big water. They had come on foot and would depart on foot. The boats had been prepared for the brides. It was the custom that they be brought to their new village by their own people. And now the brides stood on the shores of the lake and watched their grooms depart. When the last of the guests had disappeared around the bend, the farewells with the brides began.

They seated themselves in the boats two by two. The oldest women went with them so they could themselves hand the young girls over to the care of the older women in their new home.

The oarsmen lifted their oars and the boats floated away over the quiet water. The women remained on the shore for a long time, their tearful wails making a kind of song.

A year would pass and the same song would be repeated on the same shores.

But of all the women, Laughing One shed the bitterest tears. The women thought she cried because of the loss of Echo, who was as close to her as a sister, but no one suspected that an even greater loss was imminent. Bei and Liok had decided to leave the following day. They had told Laughing One that this was the most convenient day—everyone would be sleeping after the long festivities and the tearful departure of the brides, and no one would notice their leaving. Bei had once more tried to talk Laughing One into leaving with them, but she had said, "Echo is going away. You and Liok are going away. How can I leave Kru? The old man loves and cares for us all. What will become of him if he is left all alone? I must stay."

Chapter 13

THE DAY FOLLOWING the departure of the brides the village appeared deserted. No one went for water, no one went out for firewood. The children had scattered early in the morning in search of berries, while the adults slept. Even the dogs, sated from the leftovers of the three-day feast, slept soundly in the shade of the huts.

It was quiet in Kru's hut. Kru himself and his grandson snored serenely on their soft skins. Bei tried once again to convince Laughing One to go with them.

"How can I leave?" she repeated. "How can I leave the old man?"

Bei had hoped vainly that when it came time for them to leave she would change her mind. They sat for a long time, heads lowered, not looking at each other. Finally Bei rose slowly, patted the sleeping boy on his curly locks, carefully touched Kru's gray head in a gesture of farewell, and once again for the last time looked at Laughing One, the unspoken question in his eyes. She understood the silent question and silently motioned to the sleeping ones. Bei's last hope was crushed. He turned and quickly walked out of the hut and went to the hut of the masters.

Kibu, a great lover of the "happy drink," was sleeping soundly. Liok was sleeping too, though Bei woke him with the lightest touch. Liok had everything ready—in a leather pouch he carried his two favorite hammers and a store of smoked meat for the long journey. Liok could not bring himself to look at the sleeping Kibu. He was sorry to leave the master and his hut. At the same time the thought of returning home filled him with joy.

Bei had decided that it would be wisest for them to travel at first along the shallow waters of the lake, so that in case of a chase the dogs would not catch their scent. They came out to the water of the lake. But as they stood looking around them for one last time, they noticed spots on the water in the distance. At first they seemed immobile, barely visible, then their size increased.

"Can they be returning already?" said Liok in surprise. "But they are not expected until tomorrow."

"It is not the old women," said Bei slowly. "These boats belong to strangers."

"Enemies?" said Liok anxiously.

"Yes. Enemies," answered Bei, "so you and I will not run away after all. These people have made us their sons. We will not leave them in their peril. Go wake the Glavni. I will wait here."

It was difficult to wake the Glavni, but when he finally heard the word "enemies," he rose from his stupor. Quickly they wakened the village. The old men led the women and children to a hideaway in the swamps, while the hunters, armed with spears, axes, and bows and arrows, headed toward the lake. They arrived on the shore still in time.

The invaders sailed into shore and drew their two long boats onto the beach. They walked up and down the beach looking about carefully. They were tall with long blond hair and were dressed in jerkins made of walrus skin. Each one carried a long shiny stick tied to his side. Laughing and shouting they dragged a woman out of one of the boats onto the shore. Her hands were tied behind her, her clothes were torn, and her face bruised and bloody. It was Echo!

An angry murmur passed through the hunters hidden in the lakeside bushes, but the Glavni silenced them with the call of a sea gull. A man, who held Echo by the ends of the ropes that tied her hands, pushed her forward. The girl turned her tormented face in the direction of the village, then turned and walked away from it. The fair-haired men took their shiny sticks in their hands and followed behind Echo in a single file. The Glavni counted the fingers on both hands four times before all the strangers were counted. There were not as many hunters in the whole village.

It would have been foolish to jump out on the open beach—better to lure the strangers into the forest and attack them from behind bushes and tree trunks. Perhaps Echo would lead her tormentor to the traps hidden in the forest.

No mistake! Echo was headed directly toward the traps. How deceptive was the stillness of the forest! The tall warriors walked silently along the narrow path. On either side, unseen by the enemy, were Echo's kinsmen. Some of them stole behind the strangers, while others hurried toward the trap to meet them there in face-to-face combat.

Echo stopped at a turn in the path. Beyond her lay the cleverly hidden traps. She fell to the ground and in spite of a shower of rough kicks, she would not move. Kru and his sons leapt forward at that moment, and two yellow-haired men fell under Bei's ax. The others defended themselves with their flat shiny sticks—bronze swords!

These were terrible weapons—with one blow they could cut through the thickest pole. And Bei found that he was no longer holding a spear but a stick. But the hunters kept at the yellow-haired strangers, stabbing them with their spears and chopping at them with their axes. The strangers kept moving back closer and closer to the hidden traps. A loud shout pierced the air as one of the enemy was crushed in the traps. Then another and another. Squeezed into the narrow forest path, with the traps at one end, the strangers were having a hard time of it. Finally, the tall bearded leader shouted out something, and the yellow-haired men started to make a run for the lake.

Kru lifted Echo in his arms, wanting to move her from harm's way, but the leader of the invaders raised up his sword and Kru lay dead with his arms around the mortally wounded Echo. So great was Bei's rage when he saw what had happened that he killed the yellow hair with a single blow of his broken spear shaft. Then grabbing the sword from the dead man, he struck a man behind him on the neck with it. The enemy's head rolled to Bei's feet. "Surely," Bei thought, "there is magic in the power of this strange weapon."

Although the path was narrow and crooked the strangers never left it, for fear of getting lost in the unknown woods. Many people of the village and many more yellow-haired strangers parted with their lives along that path before the fighting was over. Forty strangers had landed on the shores of the lake, and now they numbered less than ten. Vainly they called to the rest of their number, but no more yellow-haired men came out of the forest.

The people of the village had also suffered high losses. The swords of the strangers had inflicted mortal wounds on whomever they touched.

The Glavni ordered his men to remain hidden in the bushes so as not to show the strangers how few men were left.

The strangers got into a boat and slowly moved away

from shore. It was still possible to catch up with them in one of the lighter boats, and Bei shouted, "We must not let them get away, they will come back in greater number! Our spears are longer than their shiny sticks."

"Their shiny sticks cut our spears in half," answered the Glavni grimly. "We have lost too many men."

But Bei could not accept this. He cried out hotly to the men, waving his new sword in the air, "We can still catch them. Who is not afraid to come with me?"

"Drop the weapon of the enemy. It will bring us bad luck," ordered the Glavni.

"I have already killed four men with it," answered Bei, "and I will use it to kill the others."

He ran to the place in the bushes where their boats were hidden. But the Glavni blocked his path. "Who dares to go against the Glavni?" he roared.

"I dare!" answered Bei. "The strangers will bring more enemies upon us, and we will all perish." And turning to his brother he said in their tongue, "Follow me!"

The two brothers carried one of the light fast boats to the water.

"Who else will go with us to kill the enemy?" shouted Bei, and three more hunters joined the two brothers.

The little boat easily caught the escaping enemy, but Bei realized that they could not fight the men from their own boat, for one blow from a heavy oar would sink them.

"I will jump over into their boat and fight them with the shiny stick," shouted Bei, "while you throw your spears at them."

No one really ever understood what happened then. The fighting was fast and brutal, and in the end there was not a yellow-haired man left alive.

The people of the village began to count their losses.

They were very great. The mutilated bodies of their kinsmen lay on the narrow path where so recently the battle had raged. Twenty brave hunters would never again take up their spears.

But there were many dead enemies as well. They dragged forty yellow-haired bodies into a clearing in the forest. An enemy, even when dead, is still dangerous.

Not far from the clearing was a lush green swamp. The people of the village knew how deceptive its beauty was, for the swamp was quicksand and swallowed any animal or person who ventured into it. That is where they took the bodies of the enemy.

When the last body had disappeared into the slimy depths, the shaman of the village shouted, "May your spirits never depart from your bodies! May you rot forever in this swamp." The hunters repeated these words three times and then returned to the shores of the lake.

Chapter 14

IT WAS NOW time to celebrate the departure of their own dead. The leave-taking must not be a sad one, and the dead must be given food and "happy water," and dressed for the occasion.

The slain hunters were all carried to the place of the totem pole. A railing was erected and the bodies were all leaned up against it in a row, dressed now in their finest attire. The dead warriors were given bows and arrows to hold in their laps.

The hunters sat in a closed circle, and the women sat in another circle around the body of Echo. Her torn wedding clothes were patched up as well as possible, and a crown of flowers hid the bruises on her face.

The people's grief was so great that all messages for their ancestors were forgotten. The hunters sat with their dead in grim silence, and the women held back their sobs as best they could. Almost all had lost either a son or a husband.

Only when the rays of the sun had painted the tops of the spruces with crimson did the people of the village stagger back to their huts. The dead remained sitting in the clearing under the protection of the large carved pole. Tomorrow the living would return to bury their dead.

In the morning when Liok awoke, Kibu was already sitting at his polishing stone. The old man turned his bearded face to Liok and said, "Our village has lost half of its hunters, and you are still planning to return to your homeland with Bei!"

Liok became so confused that he could not say a word. He became cold all over as if he had jumped out of a warm hut into the snow.

"Who told you?" he whispered, unable to lie, but thinking with horror of what would happen to them now.

"You, yourself," answered the old man, with the same reproach in his voice.

"I have never told anyone about it!"

"At night, in your sleep, you tell me about everything, everything you have done or thought about during the day. Where did you take the two hammers yesterday?"

Liok said nothing.

"Tell me, Mon-Kibu. An old man is asking you."

Liok told him how he and Bei had started to leave the day before, and how they had seen the boats and stayed to fight the invaders.

"I thought as much when I saw you come running with the news," said the old man. "Your brother is a great warrior. He has saved us from destruction."

The old man was silent for a long time, then finally said, "Go tell Bei that he should postpone his plans to leave for a while. The hunters are displeased with the Glavni. We will hold council today."

Liok headed for Kru's hut. When he entered and saw the places where Kru and Echo had recently slept, tears came to his eyes. He wiped them away quickly with his fist and said to Laughing One, "The little rabbit has big ears." The woman quickly sent her son out for firewood, and Liok, embarrassed, told her and Bei how Kibu had discovered their plan. "The master has counseled us not to leave yet."

Laughing One was worried. "It is bad that the old man has discovered your plan. A terrible punishment awaits you if he decides to tell the others."

"He will not say anything," answered Liok quietly, "he wishes us no harm."

The three sat quietly for a long time lost in thought. Toward midday they went with the others to bury the dead.

That evening all the people gathered in the clearing in the village. It was painfully obvious how many men they had lost. The women looked anxiously at the handful of men—if more enemies came, there would be few warriors to defend them.

The hunters were loudly singing Bei's praise for not allowing the enemy to escape, and they made derogatory remarks about the Glavni.

"Do you want to be Glavni?" whispered Liok to his brother in their own language.

"I want to return to our homeland," answered Bei, barely moving his lips. "You are the clever one, think of something to tell them."

Liok looked at his brother and shook his head hopelessly.

Finally, when one of the hunters shouted out that Bei should be made the new Glavni, Kibu stepped forward and said, "Those are good words. Bei is indeed a great warrior. But we must face the fact that we do not have enough hunters among ourselves. Before our boys turn to men, many years will pass, and the enemy could strike again at any time. I think we should send Bei and Mon-

Kibu back to their homeland. If any of their kinsmen have survived, let the brothers convince them to come and live with us. We will help to feed them, and they will help to protect us from our enemies."

As the old man expected, both the Glavni and the brothers approved of the plan wholeheartedly. Bei, overjoyed, agreed instantly and loudly.

"Let Laughing One come with us," said Bei. "The women will sooner listen to another woman."

Everyone looked at Laughing One, and it was clear by her smiling face that she was in agreement.

"Let her son remain with us," said one of the old men. "The mother's heart will bring her back to her son, and she will bring back with her all who wish to come."

Laughing One's face was worried. But Kibu took her aside and said quietly, "Do not grieve. I will look after the boy. Even if something should happen and you do not return, the boy will grow into a fine hunter."

And again, as once before, the two brothers faced a long journey together. They crossed trackless swamps, and traveled through overgrown forests where no paths lay, but the thought of their goal lent wings to their feet and joy to their hearts. They were going home.